Noah strode toward Grace's room.

He'd had her on his mind all night. And strangely, when Ruth had come to relieve him the previous evening, he had been disappointed, reluctant to leave this fragile woman.

Quietly he pushed open the door to Grace's room, careful in case she was asleep. His breath caught as he saw her unbandaged face for the first time. Aware from her chart that the damage was limited to the right side of her face, he'd left instructions with the charge nurse to leave the other side exposed so that air could reach the skin.

However, Noah wasn't expecting the lovely lines of the undamaged side of her face. Due to his speciality, he was accustomed to meeting beautiful women. But this was different. Grace Stanton was different.

Even so, she would think he was either crazy or lying if he told her he thought she was beautiful. But that's what he saw.

A beautiful woman.

BONNIE K. WINN

is a hopeless romantic who's written incessantly since the third grade. So it seeemed only natural that she turned to romance writing. A seasoned author of historical and contemporary romance, her bestselling books have won numerous awards. *Affaire de Coeur* chose her as one of the Top Ten Romance Writers in America.

Bonnie loves writing contemporary romance because she can set her stories in the modern cities close to her heart and explore the endlessly fascinating strengths of today's woman.

Living in the foothills of the Rockies gives her plenty of inspiration and a touch of whimsy, as well. She shares her life with her husband, son and a spunky Westie terrier who lends his characteristics to many pets in her stories. Bonnie's keeping mum about anyone else's characteristics she may have borrowed.

PROMISE OF GRACE

BONNIE K. WINN

Love Inspired

Published by Steeple Hill Books™

STEEPLE HILL BOOKS

Steeple
Hill®

ISBN 0-373-87229-1

PROMISE OF GRACE

Visit us at www.steeplehill.com

Printed in U.S.A.

Behold, I tell you a mystery;
we shall not all sleep, but we shall all be changed.
—*1 Corinthians* 15:51

For my father, George Yedlovsky,
for making me reach and assuring me
nothing was beyond that reach. I love you, Daddy.

Prologue

Houston, Texas

Wonder wasn't always a good thing.

Not when it was all you could do.

Grace Stanton tentatively tried to reach out, but she wasn't able to feel anything because of the thick layer of bandages wrapped around her hands. Even that small movement hurt. Yet she couldn't stop herself.

Just as she couldn't stop the wondering. How had she come to be in the hospital? What was beneath the bandages? And why had this happened now with the wedding only a week away?

Aunt Ruth hovered, her eyes dark with concern. ''Grace, can you hear me?''

"Yes." The word formed in her mind, but emerged as little more than a croak.

Ruth looked as though she was about to cry. And again Grace wondered. Only this time it was mixed with dread.

"The other driver and his family are going to be fine," Ruth finally managed, her voice a bit shaky, "because of your sacrifice. If you hadn't driven into that concrete barrier when they drifted into your lane, none of them would be alive."

Grace wanted to ask questions—about the crash, her injuries…but she couldn't summon her voice. Instead she blinked her eyes.

In turn, Ruth swiped hers.

Exhausted and confused, Grace wanted to comfort her aunt, but mind and body refused to cooperate. And the beeping and whooshing of all the machines frightened her.

Ruth, who had taken Grace's parents' place after they died, leaned forward. "I know you're scared, Gracie. But remember, the Lord is with you. He'll take care of you."

Tears collected in Grace's throat. Unable to shed them, she began to wonder yet again. Was He really with her? She'd been uncertain about that since her mother and father had died.

A procession of nurses and technicians rotated through the room. Grace was relieved that they didn't expect a response from her, instead speaking to her aunt, some poking and prodding, others simply making notations.

Her aunt leaned close. "Gracie, the doctor's here."

Although her eyes were swollen, she opened them, studying the man.

"I'm Dr. Jamison, Miss Stanton. And you've had quite a bang-up." He studied the chart. "Which means you're going to be with us for a while. Your internal injuries are manageable, but you're in for a number of restorative surgeries."

She held up one of her heavily wrapped hands in question.

"You've severed a tendon in your right hand. But don't dwell on that. Many people find they can compensate very well by using their left."

She gasped. She knew that her injuries were significant, since Ruth had driven from where she lived in the small town of Rosewood to be with her in Houston. But Grace hadn't guessed how bad the injuries were. To think she wouldn't be able to use her hand—

The doctor's words interrupted the thought and jarred her at the same time. "I understand your hand isn't your major worry. But we'll have to wait for the results of the first plastic surgery to determine how much of your face can be repaired."

Terrified, she turned slitted eyes, searching for her aunt.

Ruth stepped forward, her look censoring the doctor. "Grace hasn't been awake long enough to be told how much recovery time to expect."

The doctor scratched his balding head. "Sorry to be blunt, but this is an extremely busy hospital, Miss Stanton. Our touch may not be very personal but trust me, it's extremely skilled. It may take you some time to adjust to the gravity of your injuries, but that's also normal. Don't be discouraged. You're in for a lengthy process, but you'll have to take it a day at a time. I'll be back to check on you this evening." Dr. Jamison carried the chart with him as he exited.

Ruth laid a very gentle hand on Grace's shoulder. "It'll be all right, dear. There's a lot to take in at once. Don't worry. We'll sort everything out."

A nurse entered before she could reply, injected something into one of the many tubes, and Grace felt herself fade.

When she awoke hours later Grace struggled to speak, and one word emerged, raw but audible. "Patrick?"

Ruth appeared swiftly at her side. "He's not here yet, Grace. He called the nurses' station a short while ago and he should be here any minute. It took a while for his office to reach him, but he headed here as soon as he heard.''

Grace had to know. ''What will he think?''

Ruth's chin firmed. ''He'll be worried about you, I'm sure. But he loves *you*, not your face.''

Grace closed her eyes. Unknowingly Ruth had confirmed Grace's worst suspicions. Holding on to consciousness, she heard more footsteps nearing the bed.

As she opened her eyes, her fiancé, Patrick Holden, paused at the end of the bed.

Relief started to warm her. But then it faded. And in that sickening moment she realized she no longer had to wonder. She knew. It was written on Patrick's stricken face.

''Grace...'' Patrick stared at her in horror for an instant, then shuttered his eyes so she couldn't read them.

She wanted him to come closer, to stand by her in every sense. And after a moment's hesitation he approached, his expression sorrowful.

Ruth slipped quietly from the room.

Patrick leaned close, his manner changing abruptly, becoming hearty. ''You're going to get better. I know it's scary right now, but doctors can do so much now for... Well...doctors can work miracles.''

Grace blinked yes, again struggling to speak. "Why now?"

Patrick looked blank.

"Our wedding," Grace whispered, thinking of the picture-perfect day that she had been planning for months. Actually years; she'd dreamed of this day since she was a child.

"Don't worry, Grace. We can postpone it. Everyone will understand why." He smiled too brightly. "Then you can have the fun of picking out new invitations and flowers. You know how much you enjoyed that. You're like a kid in a candy shop with all the wedding preparations."

She could see, despite his show of bravado, that he was overwhelmed. Grace found her voice; however, it was still a mere whisper. "But it's not candy. It's bad, Patrick."

He reached for her hand, then paused when he saw the thick bandages. After an awkward moment he patted her shoulder. "It's okay, Grace. We'll get through this."

Grace met his eyes, trying to see beyond the forced cheerfulness of his words. And there she saw apprehension and fear. "It won't be that easy."

He swallowed visibly. "The doctor says you've got a lot of surgeries ahead of you, that it's going to take a long time to recover. You'll have to be patient…we'll have to be patient."

Patrick was giving his best, saying all the right words. But there was no fire in his eyes or determination in his voice. And somewhere deep inside, she knew he wouldn't stand the test. How strange that it took something like this to show her his true mettle. Awash in pain and despair, she slowly shook her head.

"Grace, you can't give up. I...I know how difficult this is for you." He paused, clearly in far over his head. "I don't know what else to say."

But what he couldn't say was plastered over his perfect face. And she recognized the other emotion in his expression. Pity. He stared at her with unrelenting pity.

And beneath the swaddle of bandages, she flinched. Yet she had to know it all. She couldn't stand to wonder about anything else. "Do you still want to get married?"

His pause was barely perceptible. "Grace, we weren't expecting anything like this. It's going to take adjustments...for both of us."

And something inside Grace that the accident couldn't reach to damage suddenly crumpled.

"I'm sorry," Patrick continued. "I'm probably saying all the wrong things. Truth is, I don't know what to say."

I do. Even though you're fighting it, I see it. Grace wasn't sure she would ever view him in the same light again. And she wondered how the breaking of her heart could be so silent. There should be a great crashing noise, louder than cymbals, more wrenching than a bitter blast ripping apart the tallest structure.

He patted her shoulder again. "Things will look better as time goes by."

She pushed herself to speak past the tears collected in her throat. "I'm tired."

Patrick looked immediately remorseful. "Of course you are. You need to get some rest. I'll stop talking and just sit with you."

Somehow her heart continued to limp on despite its mortal wound. "There's no need. Ruth will be here."

"Are you sure?"

Relentlessly sure. "Yes."

"All right, then. I'll be back in the morning. You'll see. Things will look better after some time." He leaned forward, then slowly pulled back. "I'd kiss you goodbye, but I don't want to hurt any of your wounds." More pity filled his eyes. "I hate that you've been hurt like this."

Knowing how eager he was to be away from her, Grace couldn't bear to respond. Instead she half closed her painfully swollen eyes.

Patrick turned away, quickly looking back one more time before walking away. The door closed behind him as the first hot tear dampened the gauze covering her cheekbones. The tears turned to sobs, ones that pulled at her wounds, both emotional and physical.

As her sobs finally dwindled, the room became unbearably silent. Then Ruth pushed open the door. "Grace?"

"He's gone."

"I know, Gracie. But he'll be back tomorrow. I'll be here, too. And don't forget, the Lord's always with you."

Grace gathered the last of her draining energy. "Is He?"

Ruth didn't wince at the bitter question. "Yes. But I know it's hard for you to see that right now."

Everything rushed at Grace and she couldn't control the sobs. "My life is over."

Ruth cradled her as much as possible without pressing against Grace's injuries. "No, sweetie. It's just beginning. I'm going to take you home with me to Rosewood." Silently Ruth vowed to do everything in her power to help her beloved niece. "We have a wonderful plastic surgeon, Noah Brady. All the big-city hospitals are always trying to lure him away. But Rosewood's his hometown and he's staying put. It might be easier for you there, all things considered. And we'll see things through." She patted her niece's shoulder. "Don't give up hope, Gracie."

Hope. That was gone. Along with Patrick and her faith. Everything was gone. Including the wonder.

Chapter One

Rosewood, Texas

Noah Brady reread the last pages of Grace Stanton's already massive chart. The woman had been through a horrendous experience. While he'd worked on equally damaged people, this case brought his own memories close to the surface. And instinctively he knew Grace had even more pain ahead of her.

He remembered Ruth Stanton's call from Houston, her plea for his help. Despite knowing her for most of his thirty-three years, Noah had never heard her cry before. But she had broken down, her love for her niece cracking through her usual resolute demeanor.

Since the call, Noah had been consulting with Grace's attending physician. She had already been through four surgeries to repair internal injuries. Her surgeon was convinced that she wouldn't require further operations for those injuries. But her restorative plastic surgeries would be extensive.

Now that Grace was stable and her internal injuries on the mend, she was being airlifted to the small Rosewood hospital. A short time ago he'd been apprised that the helicopter would be setting down soon.

Although the hospital staff could capably transport her from the landing pad, Noah wanted to be there. Ruth had phoned him that morning, worried because she didn't want to leave Grace on her own to be loaded into the helicopter. But by staying with her, Ruth wouldn't be able to drive back to Rosewood fast enough to outpace the helicopter. So Noah had promised Ruth that he would personally greet her niece and situate Grace in a room.

Rising from his desk chair, Noah made his way from his office in the building adjacent to the hospital. He bypassed the core of the hospital, heading to the emergency-room exit. The helipad was located just beyond the ambulance driveway.

Although Rosewood wasn't in the hub of a medical center, Noah had worked hard to ensure that the facility had what was needed for the small town.

Since he had turned his back on his lucrative job in Houston, it had taken a lot of fund-raising to keep the community hospital current.

As he walked outside, Noah could hear the distinctive whir of the incoming helicopter. As it approached, winds from the blades flattened thickly leaved branches and sent errant spring buds scattering.

Accustomed to the forceful currents, Noah didn't blink as the wind slicked back his hair and tugged at his lab coat and scrubs while the helicopter landed. His concentration was focused on the woman inside the copter.

Grace had been sedated for the journey, and as expected, she was nearly obscured by heavy bandages. Despite her medication, the jolting of the stretcher as it hit the ground must have jarred her.

Grace's eyes flew open. And as Noah looked into their blue-gray depths he saw terror. When she noticed him, the look changed, hitting him with unexpected force. It was a raw plea.

Unable to resist the compelling pull of her gaze, he let her know with his own eyes that she'd made the connection. Then he nodded, guessing she wouldn't be able to hear him clearly with the noise from the copter and the barrier of her bandages.

He walked beside her as the attendants rolled her inside. Noah made sure he was in her line of vision as they took the shortest route to the room that had been readied for her.

Although he could easily prescribe more medication that would sedate her, he wished there was another way to erase the fear and uncertainty in Grace's eyes. Ruth hadn't indicated whether there was anyone else to stand by her niece. But Noah's instincts told him that Grace Stanton was alone except for her aunt.

Once Grace was settled in a bed, her vitals taken and recorded, Noah adjusted the blinds and the overhead lights so they wouldn't glare into her eyes. He saw her lids flicker in relief.

And it occurred to him that he hadn't yet heard her speak. Her records hadn't indicated damage to the vocal cords, but he wondered if emotional trauma was silencing her.

''Grace?''

She didn't answer right away. Instead she lifted her eyelids with what seemed to be great effort. ''Yes.''

Her voice surprised him—the clarity, the bell-toned sound of the single word.

''I'm Dr. Brady.''

''Ruth told me about you.''

Despite his usual reserve, he smiled, lifting his eyebrows. ''I doubt you could have stopped her.''

Surprise lit her eyes.

The past had taught Noah to maintain only a professional relationship with his patients, yet he wanted to put Grace at ease. "I've known your aunt since before she started planting blackberries."

"Blackberries?" Grace echoed.

Seeing her focus on something other than her pain, he continued. Besides, with the medication he'd just diagnosed, he was fairly confident that Grace wouldn't remember his words. "I told her the pears on her tree weren't worth snitching. The next spring she planted blackberries. Over the years she's complained how they sprawled out in the yard, climbing up her ivy lattice and taking over." He grinned, remembering that easy time. "They're so big, one berry fills your mouth. Better than caviar. And to this day Ruth hasn't ripped them out. Between you and me I think she likes knowing she can make the best blackberry pie in town."

A fraction of relief eased into Grace's eyes. He guessed few people still spoke to her as though she might enjoy a normal conversation.

"Her pie's the best," Grace finally replied.

"This is making me hungry. Do you feel like eating?"

"No." The word was small, seeming to match her damaged spirit.

"Have you had much appetite since the accident?"

She sighed. "The doctor questions begin."

Noah studied her, having acquired a second sense about victims. He didn't need to see her expression to guess what it would reveal. "Had enough of those already?"

She nodded.

"You're going to have a lot more," he told her. His tone was uncompromising, but she needed to hear the truth. "We're going to be a team, Grace. But I can only function as the captain if you're an able navigator."

Her eyelids closed again.

He recognized the action as a defense, one he'd seen many times before. Noah turned away. But an inner voice nagged him to turn back. And his words seemed to come from a source he no longer thought he possessed. "I'll make you a deal. You drink your broth and I won't ask you any more questions today."

It took a moment, then she nodded.

Noah made a quick, unprecedented decision. Leaving Grace, he called the cafeteria. It took only a few minutes for a worker to bring up the tray from the kitchen.

Grace was resting quietly when he returned to her room. He adjusted her bed carefully, knowing her body was a mass of pain. Once the broth was in place on her bed table, Noah situated the straw.

Then he pulled up a chair, placing the tray across his knees. He'd only spent this much nonwork-related time with his young patients. And still then, he kept his distance. Not because he didn't care, but because he'd learned his lesson well in the past.

Grace glanced over at him, then down at the loaded tray. "I can't eat all of that."

"I'm pleased to hear it. This is *my* dinner."

Surprise lit her eyes again.

"You don't mind my eating with you?" he asked, retrieving a french fry, acting as though he routinely shared dinners with patients.

Cautiously she shook her head.

Noah ripped open a packet of ketchup. "Hospital life can get somewhat intrusive. It's difficult to make a phone call or eat a meal without interruption. People assume if you're a doctor you don't have a life." He took a bite of his hamburger. As he swallowed, he acknowledged how true that was. His complete commitment to the hospital only emphasized the empty holes in his life.

"I never thought of that," Grace replied softly.

He was pleased that she had offered a complete reply. "Most people don't. But you take the good with the bad. When I first decided that I wanted to be a doctor I didn't think it was possible." Pushing away the difficult memories, he stood, placing his tray on the bedside table. "You're not keeping up your part of the bargain." Grasping the straw, he held it up to her mouth. Seeing she wasn't motivated to eat, Noah hoped it wasn't an indication of a complete loss of will. "You don't want me to start the inquisition again, do you?"

Her eyes, darkening pools of sorrow, met his.

An unexpected fist of emotion clobbered him. The danger that feeling held made him pause. But he couldn't ignore the agony in her eyes. "Can you manage a small sip?"

She parted her lips.

Noah held the straw for her. She drank about a teaspoonful of the broth. Even that movement seemed to fatigue her.

"It's okay, Grace. Your appetite will return as you heal. I'll keep prodding you so the healing process goes more quickly." He gently encircled an uninjured patch of her forearm. "We're in this for the long haul, Grace."

A new uncertainty flashed in her eyes.

Noah wondered why she had no one except Ruth to care for her. Was it possible she had no family? No special man in her life to stand beside her?

As Noah watched, Grace moved the fingers on her left hand, the less injured of the two.

Momentarily ignoring his own defensive instincts, he grasped her outstretched fingers.

While the noise of carts rattling down the hall and

the paging of doctors persisted outside the room, Noah continued to watch her.

A solitary tear escaped from her tormented eyes. Noah gently wiped it away, the echo of the busy hospital receding. And her fingers cautiously tightened around his.

The pit of his stomach tightened. It was his duty as her doctor to heal her. It was his duty to himself to remain uninvolved. At all costs.

Chapter Two

The lights were bright. But they always seemed that way since the accident. Grace watched the nurse's expression as the woman carefully unwrapped the bandages covering her face.

Most of the professionals who had performed this task hadn't commented on the condition of her face. Grace supposed it went with the medical training. *Don't let the patient know she looks grotesque.*

Grace knew she should be accustomed to the process, but it wasn't getting any easier. If anything, it had become more and more difficult as the reality sank in.

"You're lucky," the nurse declared.

There was that word again. The same one her new

doctor had used before he left. That blackberry doctor with the gentle but supportive touch.

''The left side of your face has a few scratches remaining, but the bruising and swelling has diminished from what's noted last on your chart in Houston.''

Part of Grace wanted to reach up and touch the allegedly undamaged portion of her face. A larger part of her couldn't stand the awfulness. She supposed half a face was better than none, but it was difficult to be grateful for that small reprieve. And so she remained quiet as the nurse continued the bandage change.

Grace was surprised to feel coolish air against her exposed cheek when the nurse started to leave. ''Aren't you going to finish?''

The nurse smiled. ''I did.''

Grace still couldn't bear to touch her cheek. Instead she leaned the bandaged side of her face against the pillow. It all seemed so unreal, so unbelievable.

Occasionally she still dreamed that everything was all right. And in the brief moments as she awoke she would feel the relief of knowing the accident wasn't real. But then the darkness set in.

Other times she would dream of Patrick's face, remembering his halfhearted attempts to deal with her injuries. And the bitterness of her waking hours invaded the deep of night, as well.

. She had expected Patrick to stand beside her. Not motivated by obligation, but rather strength and love. But he'd folded in the first instant. How had she misjudged him so?

Perhaps no such man of strength existed. Wasn't love supposed to bear all things? She needed Patrick to say he loved her no matter what, not to set a new world's record for coming up with excuses.

He hadn't spoken of visiting her in Rosewood. He had muttered something about business commitments. Besides, she would be in the hospital, undergoing numerous surgeries, he'd added.

He had suggested she might prefer to have Ruth with her during this difficult time. But Grace had seen through the excuses. Patrick wanted her to disappear, to take the ugliness she had become out of his well-ordered life.

Closing her eyes, Grace listened to the sound of footsteps in the corridor, wondering if any of the technicians or doctors were headed her way. Ones like the blackberry doctor. Silly to think of him like that. But he was the only medical professional Grace had encountered who hadn't treated her as though she was only a mound of bandages.

She didn't place any value in his words or actions, though. It was simply his job. Beyond that, he was a man.

The following day Noah strode toward Grace's room. He'd had her on his mind most of the day. And strangely, when Ruth had come to relieve him the previous evening, he had been disappointed, reluctant to leave this fragile woman. It was an atypical reaction for him. He couldn't survive becoming involved again.

Quietly he pushed open the door to Grace's room, careful in case she was asleep. His breath caught as he saw her unbandaged face for the first time. Aware from her chart that the damage was limited to the right side of her face, he'd left instructions with the charge nurse to leave the other side exposed so that air could reach the skin.

However, Noah wasn't expecting the lovely lines of the undamaged side of her face. He'd met his share of beautiful women. But this was different. Grace Stanton was different.

Even so, she would think he was either crazy or lying if he told her he thought she was beautiful. But that's what he saw.

A beautiful woman.

The impression had begun with his first glimpse

of her eyes. She had spoken more with her eyes than her voice. And more than most women did with both.

This one woman struck him far more strongly than any in his memory. So much so that Grace had been in his thoughts since the previous evening and throughout his morning rounds. He'd purposely made her the last patient on his rounds in case she needed extra attention.

Grace moved her head, and he realized she was awake.

"Hello, Miss Stanton."

"Hello." Her reply was soft, hesitant.

Noah was certain Grace had long since tired of being asked how she was feeling. Instead he approached the bed, studying her exposed face carefully.

She averted her eyes.

He picked up her chart. "Did you eat your Wheaties this morning?"

She turned her face back toward him, her eyes blinking in surprise. "Wheaties?"

"Yep. You're going to have to be a champ today. I've scheduled a full day of tests."

She looked at him in silent inquiry.

"The sooner you're ready for surgery, the sooner you'll be dancing on tables."

Her eyes reproved him. "I don't do that."

"Maybe not. But you'll be able to if the whim

strikes you. The last tests you had in Houston show a marked progression. So my instincts are optimistic that we can begin surgery in a few days.''

''Oh.''

He glanced up from the chart. ''You don't sound very encouraged.''

''I don't mean to seem ungrateful. But it's difficult to be enthused.''

He met her gaze, noticing that today her eyes seemed gray. He wondered if it was a trick of light or if she possessed changeling eyes. ''I don't expect enthusiasm, Grace. You've been thrust into a life-altering experience with little time to absorb what's happened. Many of your friends probably haven't known what to say or do.''

He saw a flash of recognition.

So he continued. ''You're going to have to take the lead in your recuperation. I can captain the medical care, but if you steer us into a reef, we'll go aground.''

''I'm not feeling much like steering.''

''No. I don't imagine you are. But it does get better. It's not easy. In fact, it's frustrating and painful.''

''Don't feel you have to use kid gloves, Doctor.''

''I don't. I could tell you a lot of soothing lies, but I respect you too much. I suppose I'm making a big assumption, but I'm guessing you're made from the same stuff as your aunt Ruth. And she'd take a switch to me if I fed her cotton candy instead of the truth.''

Grace briefly closed her eyes, then met his. "You're right. But…I'm scared."

Noah gave in to his unexpected instinct to take the unbandaged portion of her left hand. "I know you are. But you're not in this alone. Your aunt Ruth has the stamina of a dozen people."

"I suppose you're right," she murmured softly, her voice cracking.

He suspected there were buckets of unshed tears in her. There would be times she needed to cry, but he couldn't let her slide into self-pity and depression. Her recovery depended on a strong spirit. "You'll probably be ready to throw rocks at me before we're through, but like I said, I'm tough."

Tough enough to disregard the appeal she evoked in him, he reminded himself, seeing her fingers curled inside his. Yes, tough enough.

Nearly two weeks later, Grace pushed at the soft, mushy food on her tray. The taste and consistency resembled baby food, since she still couldn't chew properly. Dr. Brady had promised she would be able to in the future. He had also emphasized the importance of eating so that she didn't compromise her health. Listlessly she stirred the carrot-colored section. The unappetizing hospital food certainly wasn't helping.

Dr. Brady was later than usual. He had taken to making his daily visit during the dinner hour, often eating with her. Perhaps he had decided she'd had enough personal hand-holding.

Grace couldn't repress seeds of disappointment. Funny, he was the only person who had thought to offer her physical comfort, to actually take her hand. Even though it was in his professional capacity. Patrick had looked scared to death simply to stand by her side. Ruth was afraid of hurting her. But Dr. Brady seemed to know she needed the tactile contact, the simple human connection.

As the minutes ticked by, she stirred her applesauce aimlessly. Ruth had gone home for the day. She would be back in the morning faithfully as she always was. But that left a lot of empty hours.

The door whooshed open suddenly. Noah Brady swept inside. "Hello."

"Hey," she replied, her disappointment receding.

He placed his tray on the table, then reached into a white paper sack and pulled out a large disposable cup. "Think I can talk you into a milk shake instead of the usual mush?"

"Chocolate?" she asked, her absent appetite making a revival.

He smiled, a wide grin that revealed even white teeth. "Is there any other flavor?"

"Not for me," she admitted, studying his face. "But something tells me there's more to this than ice cream."

"Ah, the lady is sharp. You're right. It's a celebration."

"For what?"

"I just finished the analysis of your last tests. You're ready for your next surgery."

Fear scorched her insides, much the way the pain of her injuries had. What if these surgeries didn't help? What if all of it was for nothing? She gasped for air as she considered the grim possibilities.

"Take a deep breath," Noah instructed.

She did. Several deep breaths, in fact.

But he didn't seem fazed.

"Sorry," she said, finally calm.

"It's okay. Plastic surgery isn't like an appendectomy. It's rarely routine, we can't always predict the outcome, and in a case like yours there's a lot riding on the success."

"Did you completely skip Bedside Manner 101?"

He smiled again. "That's more like it. Now, taste your milk shake."

She obliged. "It's good."

"Wrong. It's delicious. I'll bring you another one after surgery when you can appreciate it."

Grace awkwardly grasped the cup with her bandaged left hand. "When is the surgery?"

"Tomorrow morning."

Her eyes widened. "So soon?"

"No point in waiting."

She supposed he was right, but what if the surgery failed?

"And right now you're wondering about the outcome, whether it could be bad."

His intuitiveness took a bite out of her fear. "And if it is?"

"Then you'll most likely need even more surgeries than I'd initially believed. But that's possible anyway."

"It sounds like it may never end."

He met her eyes. "It will probably feel that way no matter how tomorrow's surgery goes."

She swallowed. The truth was harsh, but marshmallow-covered lies would be more painful in the long run. "I'm not sure I could do your job, the part about delivering the news to the patient."

"I chose this field because of the patients. It's personal to me."

"But you don't know me."

"I'm beginning to," he refuted. "Already I know you like milk shakes better than baby food."

"That doesn't count. I imagine even babies would prefer milk shakes. Tell me something else."

"You're smart. You're strong. And you have excellent taste in doctors."

She felt a smile forming despite her injuries, then glanced at the cafeteria tray he'd brought in. "Isn't your dinner getting cold?"

"I don't know the difference anymore. I'm so used to leaving meals unfinished that hot food might be a shock to my system." He glanced down at the tray. "Come to think of it, I've had so many carrots and peas it's a wonder I'm not orange and green."

"If you go on that basis, I'll be pure mush soon."

"Nope. The milk shakes will save you."

Grace suspected it would take more than milk shakes, but she didn't want to seem ungrateful for his teasing kindness. Surely he would rather be with his wife or girlfriend than pulling dinner duty in the hospital. "I'll count on it."

He swallowed a forkful of vegetables. "I called Ruth a little while ago, let her know what time you're scheduled in the morning."

"Isn't that above and beyond the call of duty?"

He tipped his head slightly. "Depends. Every doctor has his own methods."

"But doesn't that take a lot of time away from your family?"

Noah shrugged. "I see my parents when I can and they understand my reasons for a busy schedule."

"No. I meant your wife and children."

"Don't have either."

She was surprised. He seemed like the kind of man who would nurture both. "Your girlfriend, then."

"Not guilty."

Grace studied him as he took another bite of his cooling dinner. "Did you always want to be a doctor?"

"No. I was going to be a lawyer like my dad, only really big time, Ivy League, the whole works. I wanted to be the next household name in law."

That surprised her. "What happened?"

His brow furrowed. "It's a long story."

"I have nothing but time." She paused. "At least until morning."

"Remember, when you're bored to tears, you asked for this story." He paused and she could see the faraway light of memories in his eyes. "It started when I was seventeen. My mother was burned severely in a chemical explosion. Rosewood didn't have much in the way of a hospital—it really wasn't more than a clinic. There wasn't a plastic surgeon in town. And my mother needed extensive care—turned out to be more than a year of surgeries and treatment. That meant she had to be in Houston the whole time, where we found her doctor. My dad couldn't take the idea of my mother being on her own through all that, so we moved to the city.''

"That's a pretty big change for a teenager."

"Yeah. I was scared my mother would die. But at the same time I couldn't figure out where I fit in anymore. Here in Rosewood I was the star quarterback with a great future. In Houston I wasn't even bait in a large pond.''

So he knew how it felt to be the odd one out, as well.

"Then in my senior year we had a class assignment that was supposed to help us figure out what we wanted to do with our careers. We had to shadow someone in our chosen profession. Well, I didn't really have one anymore because I'd become so unfocused. Law school didn't have the appeal it had back in Rosewood.

"I couldn't go out for high school football because I had to stay home in the afternoons with my younger brothers and sisters. That meant I couldn't hope to be on a college team, which in turn meant I wouldn't be recruited by the pros.

"I went to visit my mother in the hospital, and her surgeon was there. By that time he had worked miracles with her, even though she had a long way to go. And it hit me. If Rosewood had a doctor like him, families wouldn't have to be torn from their homes, away from everything they know, to get good medical treatment.''

Grace suddenly wondered if the doctor was too good to be true. "That sounds really noble for a high schooler.''

"I didn't mention that the town took up a collection to help us with living expenses and medical care. My family wouldn't have made it without their help. Not to mention that with the accident, moving, assuming most of the care for my siblings, it was a maturing experience.''

Although still suspicious, Grace thought of her own losses. "Yes.''

"The surgeon let me shadow him. I sat in on late-afternoon rounds and appointments, surgeries. I was able to read what he charted…and it was the greatest experience of my life. I hadn't really expected that.''

"Does it still feel that way?''

He hesitated, and she sensed he was retrieving more memories. But he didn't share them, nor did he answer her question. "How about you? We've never talked about your work.''

"I'm in… I *was* a public relations rep.''

"Did you quit?''

Exasperation bubbled. "I had an accident, remember?''

"I don't see how the two are related. Unless your

employer isn't willing to hold your job until you recover.''

She flinched. ''Public relations means meeting the public.''

''I'm sure your job consists of more than appearance. What kind of firm do you work for?''

''Did,'' she insisted. Grace thought of her job, how fulfilling it had been. But returning to public speaking and networking seemed impossible. ''I worked for an independent oilman who wants to give back to the community. So he's a strong charity advocate. The biggest part of my job is...was organizing fund-raisers.'' She swallowed, remembering, hurting for what was gone. ''The fund-raisers were for causes that had become very dear to me.''

''Why should that change? Clearly they still mean a great deal to you.''

Grace remembered how she'd confidently accepted invitations to speak anywhere there was a prospect of raising contributions for the Texas Children's Hospital, cancer research and others. She couldn't imagine how she would ever resume her life—not with an endless stream of pity or disgust from the people she had once inspired to help others.

''Grace?''

Belatedly she raised her head. ''Things have changed. Even you can't pretend they haven't.''

"Of course they have. But there's a reason for everything."

"You sound like Ruth. No matter how grim things get, she insists it's in the heavenly plan."

"And you don't?" he questioned quietly.

She couldn't face those doubts right now. A promise of long ago echoed in her thoughts. An unfulfilled promise. "I don't know."

To her relief he didn't push. "You've got a lot on your plate right now. But I want you to feel good about tomorrow."

"Do most of your patients feel good about their surgeries?"

His expression darkened. "Depends. The fighters know each one is a step they have to take."

Grace looked at him with the obscured view Patrick's desertion had bred. "And you're so sure I'm a fighter?"

"I believe in you more than you do right now."

She swallowed a sudden lump of emotion. "That's not saying a lot."

"Don't underestimate me."

Grace realized suddenly that the possibility had never even been a consideration. And her doubts flared. Trusting another man, even the supposedly good doctor, could only lead to pain.

Chapter Three

Ruth's anxiety was nearly painful to watch.

"Can't I get you some coffee?" Noah asked.

"It's not me we have to worry about. This child's been through so much loss, so much pain." Ruth glanced down at Grace, who was still sleeping after her transfer from the recovery room. "The way she lost her parents...now this."

"She's strong, Ruth. She'll get through it."

"Physically. But this sort of damage is hard for a woman. It's not something I can explain."

She didn't need to. Noah knew the emotional trauma involved. "I haven't known Grace for long, but I think she's strong emotionally."

Ruth nodded slowly. "Maybe so."

"And like the previous ones, her surgery went

without a hitch. I'm very optimistic about her prospects.'' He glanced at his watch. ''Ruth, it's late and you've been here since dawn. Why don't you go home and get some rest?''

Her face was lined with fatigue. ''I need to be here if Grace wakes up.''

''I'll stay.''

''I can't ask you to do that.''

Even though Noah was regretting his impulsive offer, he couldn't withdraw it. ''Grace will really need you tomorrow. You'll do her more good if you go home and get some rest.''

Ruth took one last look at her niece. ''She's so dear to me.''

''I'll take good care of her,'' Noah promised. ''You can count on me.''

She pursed her lips. ''You've never let me down before. And I don't expect you're going to start now. I'll take these old bones home, but I'll be back first thing in the morning.''

''Good night, Ruth.''

Once she left, Noah studied Grace's sleeping form. The bandaged side of her face lay against the pillow. And even though he was well acquainted with her disfiguring injuries, he couldn't help thinking how lovely Grace looked. And how vulnerable.

Noah rarely spent this much time with a singular

patient. Not since the experience that had changed him forever.

Still, he found himself drawn to Grace.

He didn't really understand it. She'd struck a chord deep within. That alone should have told him to back off, to put extra distance in place.

Grace sighed and he stepped closer.

Her eyelids quivered with the effort of opening them. She looked at him in confusion, unfocused. She tried to speak, but her lips and mouth were dry.

Noah offered her a few ice chips.

Grace swallowed, then looked up at him again. "Blackberry doctor?" she croaked.

He smiled at the reference. "Yes, I'm the blackberry doctor. And you're doing great."

"Navigator," she managed, her voice still muffled from the anesthesia.

He took the fingers of her left hand, surprised and touched that she remembered these two things. "Yeah. And I'm the captain."

She closed her eyes briefly, then stared up at him. "Where to?"

"Sleep," he replied gently. "And you won't believe how much better you're going to feel before long."

Her eyes drifted closed again.

Good night, sweet Grace.

It took Noah longer than he expected to release her hand. And even longer to finally leave her that night.

Grace could scarcely believe it. Four surgeries later, true to Noah's promise, she was going home. Well, to Ruth's home. There would be more surgeries to repair her face, but Noah said she was ready to leave the hospital.

"It's so wonderful to see green lawns and flowers." She inhaled deeply. "And nothing smells of antiseptic. I can't wait to take a walk."

"You still have to be careful," Ruth reminded her. "Nothing strenuous for at least six weeks."

Grace knew her aunt was worried. But Grace didn't feel fragile.

"Let's go in," Ruth was saying.

She followed her aunt, who had insisted on carrying Grace's small bag. She was immediately drawn back to her childhood, the visits to this comforting home.

It had been years since Grace had been in Rosewood. Ruth had traveled to Houston for their visits and holidays. First, when Grace's mother had passed away, also spending the summers with her. Then, after Grace's father passed away, Ruth had made the trips because Grace was in college. And the custom continued when Grace became immersed in her career.

She had forgotten how warm and cozy Ruth's home was. Sunshine poured in the oversize bay window. Plump pillows in the window seat invited reading, napping, contemplating.

"It looks wonderful," Grace murmured.

"This old place?" Ruth waved away the compliment. "Pish. I don't think it's changed since you were here last."

"That's what's so wonderful."

"Never having children of my own, the furniture doesn't get worn out. No one to run and play, mess up things."

Impulsively Grace laid a hand over Ruth's. She had never realized not having children bothered her aunt. But the regret in Ruth's eyes was too clear to miss.

"Aunt Ruth, you have me. I couldn't ask for anyone dearer—you've always been there for me. I don't know what I'd have done without you. I'm sorry I've taken that for granted."

Tears misted in Ruth's eyes. "Child, you are a wonder. Let's get you settled on the couch."

Grace wanted to protest. But she *was* exhausted from the trip home. It was ridiculous, but she suddenly felt weak and wobbly. "Okay."

Ruth fussed, draping an afghan over her. "I'll make some tea."

"That sounds good, if you'll join me."

"A cup of tea wouldn't go amiss," Ruth agreed.

The sofa was situated close to the window and Grace took advantage of her position to study the view. Rosewood was a quiet town, a place where neighbors still knew each other and friends dropped by without notice. Grace touched the bandages wrapped over one side of her face, wondering just how much company Ruth usually had. While she was glad to be home, it occurred to her that she wouldn't be as protected and isolated as she had been in the hospital.

It seemed nearly unbelievable that she had been in the hospital long enough for the seasons to change. But the children playing in their yards were evidence of the passing days.

The doorbell rang suddenly.

Grace felt her muscles clench at the prospect of seeing anyone.

Ruth left the kitchen, her shoes an even tapping sound on the wooden floor as she walked to the front door, then opened it. There was a murmur of voices, then the door closed.

Ruth entered the living room, carrying an arrangement of flowers. "Now, isn't this nice."

Grace eyed the flowers warily. "Yes."

"They're flowers, not grenades." Ruth removed the card, handing it to Grace. "At least find out who they're from before reacting."

But Grace didn't need to read the card. During her hospital stay, the large, formal arrangements had come from her employer, who insisted her old job would wait for her as long as it took for her to recover. It was a kind notion, but not practical.

The roses had been from Patrick. His flowers had arrived regularly, although he hadn't. He phoned Ruth rather than her, as though scared even to speak to her. And despite Grace's long hospital stay, he hadn't made it to Rosewood. As far as she was concerned, Patrick had defected. The roses, she had decided, were to ease his conscience. And were a way to salvage his image.

Glancing at the flowers, she realized the arrangement didn't fall into either category. Fresh, vibrant daisies were nestled into an ivory Victorian vase. Curiosity compelled her to pull the card from the small envelope.

''Welcome home. Noah''

Grace wasn't sure how other plastic surgeons treated their patients, but she suspected her blackberry doctor was one of a kind. He had continued his custom of visiting her each evening, often sharing her dinnertime.

She remembered his pep talk that morning. To his credit, it hadn't sounded like the canned speech she guessed most doctors gave. But then, he wasn't like any doctor she knew.

Grace stared at her stiff right hand. Noah maintained therapy would begin this week. Despite the Houston doctors' diagnoses, Noah insisted she would regain its use. She couldn't see how.

But then she couldn't believe his other assurances, either, that she would recover, that her scars would most likely be minimal. Grace suspected it was Noah's way of being kind. But all the kindness in the world wouldn't make her whole again.

Still, she glanced down at his flowers, reaching out to touch the creamy texture of the charming vase. Grace wished she could take heart from his gesture, but sorrow had stolen her hope.

A week later, Noah felt he had given Grace enough time to ease back into life outside the hospital. Although it wasn't his custom to make house calls, Ruth had asked him to check on Grace. She had repeated the therapist's report that Grace was resisting therapy. Ruth hoped he could prod Grace into the treatment she needed.

Noah rang the doorbell and waited. It didn't surprise him when Ruth opened the door, rather than Grace.

Her worried expression lightened a bit. ''Evening, Noah. It's good to see you.''

''You too, Ruth. How's our patient?''

Ruth raised her eyebrows, then nodded her head

toward the living room, indicating Grace's presence. "Seems to be doing fine."

Noah entered the living room, his gaze going to Grace. Although she had her legs stretched out on the couch, covered by an afghan, she wasn't a picture of frailty.

Ruth followed him into the room. "Would you like some lemonade or iced tea, Noah?"

"No thanks, Ruth. Grace and I won't need refreshments."

Understanding laced with gratitude flooded the older woman's eyes. "I'll be in the kitchen."

Noah walked closer to Grace. "Hello."

"Hi." Discouragement colored her voice.

"How are you today?"

She inclined her head. "Okay, I suppose."

"And you've probably had all the fussing you can withstand."

Grace smiled faintly. "Pretty much."

"Then you should be pleased to know that I'm not here to fuss."

"Good."

"It's time for some work."

Grace looked surprised. "You might have to arm wrestle Aunt Ruth if you try to get me to do more than lie here."

"She's tough, but I'll take my chances. I want to start therapy on your hand."

Frowning, Grace held up her rigid hand. "It won't do any good."

Noah knew it was time to stop coddling her. "Let me rephrase that. It's time for *you* to work."

Even more surprise covered her face. "You say that as though I've been vacationing in the south of France."

"No. But up until now you've let others do for you. It's time you took an active part in your recovery."

Grace was beginning to rethink her opinion of the kindly doctor. There was a force in his voice and words that was nowhere near benevolent. "Doing what?"

"Today we're going to exercise your hand."

She glanced down at her motionless limb. "The therapist tried. He couldn't induce any movement."

"I can."

"How?"

He took her hand in his, gently but firmly grasping her fingers, stretching them.

The pain was excruciating and she immediately recoiled.

"Grace, this isn't going to be easy."

"You didn't say it would be killing pain!"

"I told you this would be tough. You have two choices. Give up or find the strength."

Grace fought the threat of tears. "From where?"

He met her gaze. "Everyone has a different source of strength."

She knew he meant the Lord, but she hadn't reconciled that yet.

"All right, let's stretch again," Noah instructed when she didn't reply.

"Again?"

His expression became pointed. "For a total of two so far."

"It's not easy," she protested, knowing she sounded wimpy, but not caring.

"If it were easy, it wouldn't be called work," he told her without apparent sympathy.

What had happened to the kind man who had helped her in the hospital? This tyrant had no pity.

She stared at him, frost coating her expression. "I can do it without your help."

He released her fingers.

Still angered, she stretched her hand, determined not to give in despite the pain. However, her hand didn't…couldn't move on its own. And again the pain shot through her. This time she couldn't repress the tears.

He didn't berate her as she expected. Instead, Noah gently wiped away her tears. "I know it hurts, Grace. That's why I called and asked Ruth to give you a pain pill an hour before I arrived. Is it helping at all?"

"I don't know. Maybe. But I hate acting like a wimp."

"You're not. I think it's time to strike another deal."

She glanced at him suspiciously. "I don't think even a milk shake's going to do it."

"Better than a milk shake," he promised. "We're finished for tonight on one condition."

"Anything," she agreed, knowing it was a bad bargaining strategy, not caring.

"That I come back day after tomorrow and we do at least two more stretches than today. And in the meantime, you try to stretch your hand once each morning and afternoon."

She winced. "Isn't there another option?"

"Nope."

"Then I guess I have to agree."

"I'll ask Ruth to elevate your hand on a pillow. That will help."

Grace tried not to think of the pain zinging through her hand. "Thanks."

"You'll get through this."

"If it kills me?"

Noah smiled, picking up his bag. "Well, not purposely. Goes against the oath we doctors have to take."

And despite the pain, she felt her lips twitch.

"Good night, Grace." He raised his voice. "Night, Ruth. I'll see myself out."

She watched as Noah left, wondering what he would have done if he'd been in Patrick's shoes. Throat tightening with an ache she doubted would ever heal, Grace guessed what the answer would be. After all, Noah was a man. Eyes closing, Grace acknowledged that Patrick had broken more than her heart. He'd destroyed her ability to trust.

In the following days Ruth's home remained surprisingly quiet. Grace suspected that her aunt had put a permanent hold on visitors until she could adjust to strangers.

But the transition wasn't going to be easy. The only people Grace saw were ones involved in her medical care.

Like Noah.

He had arrived a little later than she'd expected. But she could tell why. His pager hadn't stopped beeping since he had entered the house.

Noah clicked off his cell phone. "Sorry about that. It's been a crazy day."

Belatedly Grace realized she was adding to his already overloaded schedule. "Do you normally go to a patient's house?"

"Every case is different. Some need more specialized attention."

She considered that. "Oh."

"I see the wheels turning. No, that doesn't mean you aren't going to recover, just that your hand is a difficult injury. Only concentrated attention will restore your mobility."

Although knowing she probably shouldn't say it, Grace couldn't hold the words in. "All of the doctors in Houston said it would never return. How…"

"How can I be so sure I'm right?" He met her gaze. "You can believe them, or you can do the therapy. It's your choice."

She stared at her damaged hand, her voice reluctant. "The therapy."

"Have you been doing your stretches each day?"

Grace nodded. "It's hard, but yes."

He reached for her hand, carefully stretching her fingers, extending them farther than she did on her own.

Grace pulled back reflexively in pain.

Noah looked at her patiently. "We have to extend your fingers more. Holding back won't cut it."

It felt as though her hand might fall off from the pain if she did as he instructed. Grace started to protest, then saw his determined expression. So she complied.

After a few more horrendous stretches, Grace wanted to kill the once kindly doctor.

But he saved himself the gruesome fate by deciding she had done enough for the day.

Noah rummaged in his coat pocket. "Has the pain medication been adequate since you came home?"

"Until today," she admitted.

Noah handed her a few packets. "Take one of these. It's stronger and it will let you sleep tonight."

"You *knew* it was going to hurt worse today!" she said, suddenly realizing.

"This isn't my first time at the dance," he reminded her. "And don't think I'm going to be the amiable country doctor who will allow you to atrophy."

Ruth pushed open the swinging door from the kitchen. "Noah, dinner's ready and I insist you stay."

"Still afraid I'm not getting enough vegetables?" he teased.

"I know how you bachelors live." Ruth all but tut-tutted.

The smell of her fried chicken wafted toward them. Grace wondered if her aunt's exceptional cooking was going to be a deal maker.

Noah groaned. "Ruth, how can I say no to your fried chicken?"

"You can't," she replied, clearly having decided the doctor had little say in whether he stayed for dinner. Then she glanced at Grace. "You look pale, dear. Would you like a tray?"

Grace could see that Noah was awaiting her reply. Determination fused her spine. "No, you've been waiting on me enough as it is."

Ruth looked at her in concern. "Do you want a pain pill?"

"Luckily the doctor brought some with him," Grace replied, beset by a new round of stabbing pain in her hand. "They're more potent in proportion to the therapy."

Her aunt looked puzzled, then glanced at Noah.

"Therapy's rarely comfortable," he explained. "The new medication should help Grace sleep after a session."

"Ah." Ruth nodded in understanding. "I remember therapy after my back surgery." She glanced again at Grace, but spoke to Noah. "But she's doing well otherwise?"

"Yes. I'm going to have the nurse change her bandages tomorrow. They have to be done more often now—every two days."

Grace began to feel like an inanimate object. "*She's* right here."

"I'm sorry, dear," Ruth replied, obviously contrite.

Grace immediately felt ungracious. "No, I am. I didn't mean to sound like a spoiled brat."

"As though you could," Ruth told her, a note of worry still remaining in her voice.

"Yes, I can," Grace insisted, wishing she could recall the words. Instead she smiled at her aunt. "Your fried chicken smells delicious."

Ruth relaxed a fraction. "I know you like it. And I've cut up some white meat for you so it's easy to manage."

Grace withheld a grimace, hating that she had to be treated like a toddler to get by. But she couldn't say that to Ruth. "Thank you."

Ruth led the way to the dining room.

Noah hung back for a moment, his voice low, reaching only Grace's ears. "This won't last forever."

Grace wasn't so sure, but she *was* surprised that Noah had instantly read her feelings.

"And you're being a real trouper," Noah continued. "I know it's not easy to accept so much help. But you didn't let Ruth know it bothers you."

Embarrassed, she turned her eyes away. "I'm used to being an independent career woman. I've had to learn to hide a lot of my true feelings."

As Grace walked into the dining room, she missed the look of surprise on Noah's face and the reflection that replaced it.

Chapter Four

Noah glanced at the next chart, even though he knew the contents by heart. Grace Stanton was in the exam room, ready for her first post-op consultation since she'd been released from the hospital.

Thinking of the personal therapy sessions he was continuing with her, Noah walked to the exam room.

Grace looked up when he opened the door. He could see the uncertainty and fear in her eyes. Again he was struck by the emotion contained in them.

"Afternoon, Grace."

She nodded, her gaze going to the chart he held. "Afternoon."

"Still doing all right?"

"Yes." But the singular word contained a mass

of apprehension as she waited for him to examine her face for the first time since her surgery.

His fingers were sure but gentle as he removed the bandages and examined her face. The progress was as he expected. "You're healing well."

"And?"

"There's no other shoe to drop."

"So it's all good?" she questioned.

"This surgery couldn't have gone better."

She studied him closely. "And beyond *this* surgery?"

"Each surgery will be unique, but I feel confident we can expect similar progress."

"And the end result?"

He couldn't ignore her directness, nor could he tell her less than the truth. "It's possible you can completely regain your previous appearance and it's also possible that you may have residual scarring."

"Will I be a freak?" she asked bluntly.

Noah sensed the pain behind the query. "I doubt that was ever possible."

Grace shifted impatiently. "I don't want the sugar-coated version."

"That wasn't my intent." He remembered nearly identical words and emotion from years past. "Grace, we're still in the tough stages."

She swallowed, then averted her face. "Yes, I know."

He knew she considered therapy torture. Coupled with today's news, she seemed overwhelmed. He wished Grace could regain the grip on her faith. It would ease this difficult journey. But he didn't want to press and drive her further away.

"Have you gotten out of the house other than to come here?"

Startled, she looked puzzled. "No. But—"

"That's what the doctor orders. Fresh air, change of scenery."

Grace appeared horrified. "Not necessary."

"Hiding, be it in the hospital or in your aunt's home, will inhibit your recovery."

"I'm not ready to see anyone."

He took another unprofessional step. "You've already faced me. Suppose I pick you up after dinner tonight? We can take a drive." He held up his hand. "And I promise you won't have to meet any new people."

Grace studied him suspiciously. "This doesn't sound like typical doctor behavior."

He sidestepped the question, knowing he shouldn't have made the offer. "I never said I was typical. Eight o'clock?"

"I'm not sure what Aunt Ruth—"

"She's crazy about me," he interrupted, knowing she was grasping for excuses, realizing he was a fool to not let her succeed. "She won't mind."

Grace sighed. "I suppose that would be all right. But you're sure I won't have to meet anyone?"

He held up his fingers in the Boy Scout sign. But he didn't feel the responding lightness. "Cross my heart."

"Hmpf," she muttered.

Noah knew that she could easily hide away forever if she wasn't shaken out of her mode.

He also knew he wasn't the person to lead her beyond that.

Nervously Grace watched out the bay window. She had already tried to back out of the commitment, but Ruth had turned as obstinate as a hungry horse headed for the hay barn.

Convinced that the good doctor had taken her on as his "project," Grace was nearly as sure he planned to introduce her to some of the locals. And that she couldn't take.

Meeting strangers was almost as distressing as being considered a project by Noah. She'd hoped he could keep treating her like a normal person. Her hand strayed toward her bandages. But then, she wasn't normal. Not anymore.

Grace chafed at the fact that she couldn't escape this outing. Although it was comforting to be in Ruth's cosseting care, at times it also made her feel trapped. Like tonight.

A sleek Porsche pulled into the driveway and she stared in surprise. She hadn't expected him to drive something so sporty. Grace forgot about the car as she watched Noah stride to the front door.

Long and lean, he seemed very comfortable in his skin. He was handsome—she'd noticed that the first time she had seen him. It was hard to miss. Thick black hair, a bit on the long side, contrasted with his blue, blue eyes. She imagined that he attracted plenty of female attention. Yet he had said there was no special woman in his life.

The doorbell rang. Not hearing Ruth's footsteps, Grace rose. Once in the front hall, she reluctantly opened the door.

Noah's face was noncommittal.

And Grace suddenly wondered if he regretted the impulsive invitation.

She pulled the door open a bit wider. "Hi."

"Sorry I'm late," he began. "Things got pretty wild at the hospital."

"It's all right. I don't have a lot of pressing engagements."

Ruth reappeared from the direction of the kitchen. "Evening, Noah. You kids better get going if you want to have any light left."

Grace exchanged an amused glance with Noah. Funny how easy it was for older adults to reduce them to "kids" in a moment.

''Yes, ma'am,'' they chorused dutifully.

Once outside, Noah chuckled. ''I felt about ninety years old when I arrived. Nice to have some of that fall away.''

''Why so old?''

''Bad day at the hospital. I was asked to consult on a case with a disheartening diagnosis. Sorry. Didn't mean to bring my problems with me.''

''How can you not? Doctors are human, too.''

''Yeah.'' The tone of the single word was weighty, so much so that Grace searched his face, but his expression didn't tell her anything.

Noah opened the car door for her, careful to settle her in without disturbing her injuries. ''I thought you might enjoy this car more than my SUV. It's practical and roomy, but not very high on the excitement level.''

''Not something I worry about anymore.'' Still, she appreciated the fine driving machine. Grace realized she had been wrong. The Porsche suited him.

Noah drove toward the center of town. Rosewood was a charming, nineteenth-century small town that hadn't lost its appeal with the progressing centuries. False-fronted store buildings were a comforting reminder of that past.

Noah turned on to Main Street. ''I don't want to sound like a tour guide. Have you been to Rosewood often?''

"Not really. We used to visit here when I was young, then after my mother died, Aunt Ruth came to Houston. She spent the summers with me and came for all the holidays."

"How old were you when your mother died?"

"Eight," Grace told him, the memory still painful. "My dad did his best, but no one can take the place of your mother."

"Agreed. But I imagine Ruth tried."

"She did. But not in an intrusive way. Somehow Ruth knew I wouldn't welcome that. But she was great about being there for all the mother-daughter things."

"Still rough losing your mother so young."

"Doesn't really matter how old you are," Grace replied, thinking as she always did of the pain and loss associated with her mother. "You're never ready to lose them."

"What about your father?" Noah asked quietly.

"He died when I was eighteen." And she had been devastated. Another promise had died with her father, one she'd never truly gotten over.

"You had hard lessons early."

"And they keep on coming." Grace didn't want to wallow in self-pity, but she couldn't grasp why she seemed destined for tragedy.

"It seems that way right now—"

"What's next on the tour?" she asked, uncomfortable with examining such deeply emotional issues.

"Once we've exhausted the treasures on Main Street, I thought you might like to drive by the lake."

Grace had a fuzzy memory of a happy day on the lake, when her parents had still been alive. There weren't many of those memories. Her vivacious, beautiful mother had died before they could make enough of those mental-scrapbook days.

"Is that okay?" Noah asked when she didn't reply.

She pulled herself out of the past. "Sure."

Like most everything in Rosewood, it took only a few minutes to reach the lake. Noah drove slowly once they reached the gravel road that followed the shoreline; then he parked and turned off the motor.

"Why did you stop?"

He opened his door. "You'll enjoy the lake more if we're on foot."

Grace scanned the surrounding area, but it was deserted at this late hour. "Oh." Still, she was apprehensive as she left the car. She wasn't at all ready to be subjected to the stares of strangers.

The soft grassy slope beyond the road led to the shore. The only activity on the lake was the swimming of a flock of wild ducks. Rays of the surrendering sun made the water appear golden. Noah was right. It was better close up.

Grace felt a portion of her tension escape as they strolled the quiet banks of the peaceful lake. Their presence startled some birds perched nearby and they fluttered upward, taking to the sky.

Unlike so many remembered things, the lake didn't appear smaller or dimmer. The breeze was fresh, filled with the scent of the clean water.

"There's decent fishing to be had here," Noah commented.

Such a male thing, Grace thought with a smile. "Do you fish often?"

He shook his head. "Never seems to be enough time."

"Perhaps you spend too much time on your patients," she remarked pointedly.

Noah didn't meet her gaze. "It's my job."

"Doesn't leave you much time for a social life."

One of his eyebrows rose. "I manage. But there's not the mad rush of a big city to contend with here."

"That's true enough," Grace acknowledged. "It's not all bad, though. Living in the city, I mean."

"I know. I spent a lot of years in one."

"Of course. Is your family still in Houston?"

He shook his head. "We've all moved back here."

"I know you took charge of your younger siblings. Are there many in your family?"

"Five sisters and brothers."

"Whew."

Noah chuckled. "Well said. How about you?"

"I'm an only child."

Noah's expression was reflective. "You don't act like one."

"I suppose that's meant to be a compliment."

"It is."

Grace remembered words from long ago. "My father said there were two types of only children. Terribly spoiled ones who became that way because they didn't have to share either their possessions or their parents' affection with siblings and therefore considered everything solely their own. And equally generous ones, for virtually the same reason. Because they didn't have to share, or fight with siblings for what was theirs, they never felt threatened, so they were extremely generous."

Noah glanced at her. "And which type are you?"

"I guess that's for others to say."

He kept his tone benign. "You don't seem spoiled or selfish."

"Wouldn't be diplomatic of you to say so even if I were."

They passed beneath a canopy of great, green trees. "I suppose not."

Unexpectedly she laughed, realizing that was his intent.

He pointed across the lake. "See that huge oak? The one that dwarfs the others?"

She saw it easily. "Yes."

"When I was seven, two of my friends dared me to climb it. Of course I couldn't refuse. When I got really high in the branches, it was like being on top of the world. Never occurred to me that it wouldn't be so easy to climb down. I was stuck in that tree till nearly nighttime."

"Didn't someone come to help you down?"

"Eventually. My friends didn't fess up until the last minute, figuring they were going to get in trouble."

"Did they?"

"Yep. One of the rescuers was the fire chief—my friend's father."

"Ouch."

"And then some. Of course, my parents weren't real thrilled with me, either."

"But I bet it kept you out of the tree."

"For two more years."

She smiled. "Another bet?"

"Nope. Did it on my own the next time. And I almost made it down without injury."

"Almost?"

His expression was wry. "Only broke a rib. Nothing life threatening."

"Sounds like you led a charmed life."

"Sounds that way."

She remembered his mother's accident. "You liked growing up here."

"Shows, does it?"

"Only a bit."

He tossed a pebble over the bank, making it skip along the water. "It's a good place to raise a family."

Grace swallowed, thinking of her own dreams, ones that were now smashed. "Hmm."

"And it's a town where neighbors still know each other by name and look out for each other."

"Do you ever want more?" she questioned. "Rosewood's nice, but it's so small."

His lips tightened fractionally. "I came back because everything I want is here."

Grace wondered if there was a special girl he hadn't mentioned. One he hadn't yet made his girlfriend. "Then you're lucky. Most people aren't that certain."

"I wasn't always."

That seemed unbelievable. Dr. Noah Brady always appeared in control, a man who knew what he wanted and went after it. But then she'd once felt the same way.

He took her elbow. "No more deep thoughts. We've done enough excavating for one evening."

It was only after he'd taken her home that Grace realized he'd kept his word. Settling in for the night, she wondered if that was something she could count on. Then she remembered. In her new world, no man could be counted upon.

Chapter Five

Grace watched her aunt, wondering what she was up to. Ruth had been scurrying around all day.

The pit in Grace's stomach grew as she hoped her aunt's behavior didn't signal guests. Ruth had been urging Grace to allow visitors. Still raw from looks of pity while in the hospital, she wasn't ready to face new people.

The more Ruth bustled about, the more Grace worried. She was concentrating so intently that when Ruth called her name, Grace jumped. "Yes?"

"Let's go outside."

"Why?"

Ruth sighed. "It's not a surprise party, if that's what you're worried about."

Grace hid the automatic flinch. "Not exactly."

"I don't want to hurt you, child. You'll know when you're ready to let other people into your life." Ruth's wise eyes held only kindness. "And I intend to let you set the pace."

"I know you're only thinking of my best interests," Grace admitted.

"Then let's head outside." Once out of the house, Ruth went to the side of the garage and mounted the stairs that led above the structure.

Grace couldn't remember what was up there and immediately was curious.

At the top of the stairs Ruth opened a door, and they entered a well-lit room.

Grace looked around in surprise at the compact apartment that smelled of lemon oil and fresh flowers. "I didn't realize you had a garage apartment."

"When your grandmother became ill, we hired a woman to help us care for her. The apartment was hers. Since then I've used it as an overflow guest room, but that hasn't been often."

Strolling to the French doors that opened on to a small terrace, Grace glanced down at her aunt's yard and beyond. "Nice view from here."

"Do you like the apartment?"

Grace turned back around, her gaze encompassing the warm, tidy area. "It's very cozy."

"It's yours," Ruth replied, looking expectant, tremulous and nervous all at once.

"Mine?"

"If you're ready for it," Ruth explained. "I love having you in the house, but I expect since you're used to having a place of your own, you could use some quiet time without your auntie hovering."

"You don't hover!"

Ruth smiled. "Kind of you to say so, but believe it or not, I was young once."

"You still are where it counts."

Ruth's eyes misted. "And you're still the sweetest child I've ever known." She made a production of straightening a few pillows, then turned to one corner of the apartment. "The kitchen's small, as you can see. Well, everything is—even the piano's a spinet." She glanced briefly at Grace's hands. "And I'll still be cooking, so you won't have to worry about that. I freshened up everything. The colors were a bit dated, so I bought a new throw, curtains, rug and—"

"It's lovely, Ruth. The apartment and the thought. Thank you."

"You're welcome." She sniffed a bit, then turned to Grace with her usual hardy expression. "I've had the telephone man put in a separate line for you."

Grace doubted it would get much use, but she didn't want to spoil Ruth's generous gesture.

"And I've put a few treats in the fridge," Ruth continued. "The sheets and towels are fresh. And

I'll take care of the washing and tidying up. And anything else you need, of course.'' She looked around critically. ''I guess that's it.''

''I'm overwhelmed,'' Grace told her honestly.

''I want you to be sure you're ready, though.'' Ruth fussed. ''There's no hurry.''

Grace smiled. ''I think it's time to kick me out of the nest.''

Ruth raised one eyebrow. ''Sure you're ready to fly?''

''Yes. And I know where to go if I crash-land.''

Ruth looped one arm around Grace's shoulder. ''All right, then. We'll have some dinner and get you moved in.''

Grace looked at her wounded hands, unable to hide her distress. ''Oh.''

''Don't mind that. I've called in the reinforcements, just in case you were ready.''

''Reinforcements?'' Her distress multiplied.

''Noah said he'd be happy to help.''

Grace didn't know whether to be relieved that she wouldn't have to face strangers or to be exasperated because her aunt insisted on asking Noah to constantly go beyond his duties as her physician.

Glancing down at her useless hands, she tried to repress the pang that shot through her. The accident had taken more than her face—it had stolen her freedom.

It wasn't as though she'd ever been vain about her looks. She supposed she had been a nice-looking woman before, but that was simply a gift of genetics.

But she didn't know how to deal with dependence. Losing her parents so early, she'd been forced to become self-sufficient. And now it was more than a habit; it was a way of life.

Despite Noah's assurances, her right hand was still stiff, unresponsive. Again she thought of the Houston doctors, their insistence that the severed tendon wouldn't heal.

Even though she couldn't understand why Noah was so certain they were wrong, secretly she had harbored hope. But weeks of therapy hadn't made any difference.

Now she wondered if his optimistic diagnosis of her face was manufactured, as well.

"Are you ready?" Ruth's voice interrupted the thought.

Glancing up, Grace saw that her aunt stood expectantly at the door.

Ruth took a step back inside. "Is this too sudden for you? I still plan to help you with everything you can't do yet with your hands and—"

"I know I can count on you for help. I'm still having trouble with that concept, though."

Ruth nodded in understanding. "We Stantons are a strong, proud lot."

This time Grace accompanied her down the stairs. Once in the kitchen, she did what little she could to help. She could use the fingers on her left hand, even though she didn't have much strength in it yet. Hearing the doorbell, she glanced at Ruth.

"That should be Noah," Ruth said, bending over the oven, checking on the rolls. "Ask him to stay for dinner, will you?"

Grace kept the groan to herself. Still, her steps lagged as she walked to the entry hall.

Opening the front door, she gathered what composure she had. "Hello."

"Evening," he replied, his voice and manner easy, comfortable.

"Won't you come in? Ruth asked me to invite you to dinner."

His lips curved in amusement. "That was direct."

Embarrassed, Grace opened the door wider. "Sorry. But I'm afraid Ruth is asking you for too many favors."

"You mean moving your things to the apartment?" He shrugged as he entered. "She doesn't want to make you uncomfortable. I told her you were bound to grow tired of me soon and want to meet other people."

Now Grace felt thoroughly rotten. "I'm not tired of you!"

"In that case, I will stay for dinner. Do I smell homemade rolls?"

"That you do. We didn't churn the butter, however."

Noah chuckled. "What's wrong? Too much *Little House* for you?"

"Not at all. I'm getting awfully spoiled, though. Living on my own, I got used to TV dinners and takeout. Now a quick meal means a sandwich made on freshly baked bread."

"When I was about ten, I did some yard work for Ruth," Noah mused. "She paid me, then set out some lemonade and chocolate chip cookies and told me to have my fill. I ate the whole plate of cookies."

"Ooh. Stomachache?"

"A rotten one. But they were still the best cookies I'd ever eaten. But don't ever breathe a word of that to my mother."

Grace laughed unexpectedly. "I forgot you aren't a lonely bachelor to be pitied and pampered with home-cooked meals. I doubt your mother lets you starve."

"Busted," he admitted. "But I take any rescue I can get from hospital chow."

She glanced out the window at his expensive car. "Surely you can eat out in nice places."

"Yes. But Rosewood or Houston, down-home or gourmet, restaurant fare is restaurant fare."

"I suppose so."

"Do you like the apartment?"

"Very much."

"It's not too...small-town for you?"

She wrinkled her eyebrows in surprise. "Of course not. Ruth put a great deal of thought and effort into making it a cozy, welcoming place." Grace wondered suddenly if he thought she felt herself above what Rosewood offered. "*That's* it," she said aloud. "You think I'm a snob."

"No. But it's not what you're accustomed to, is it?"

Grace thought of the large apartment she'd left behind in Houston. "I've had to become accustomed to a lot of things since the accident. But I'm not attached to belongings."

"I never thought you were."

She remembered his words the evening they had strolled around the lake. He had said then that he hadn't believed her to be spoiled. "Then why do you think I look down on Rosewood?"

"Not look down. Compare."

"The two places are apples and oranges." Grace thought of her fast-paced career. There had been few quiet moments in her life in those days.

"And which do you prefer?" Noah's gaze met hers. "The apple or the orange?"

An unsettling feeling came over her. Throat dry, Grace realized that she was seeing Noah as more than just her doctor. A ridiculous pitfall, she realized. And one she couldn't indulge. Wonderful doctor or not, she was through with men.

"It's all right." He answered for her when she didn't speak. "It wasn't a fair question."

Ruth bustled in, bringing with her the aroma of the newly baked rolls. "Noah! Perfect timing. Dinner's ready. I hope you're hungry."

"Always," he replied, his voice light, sparing Grace one last glance before walking to the dining room with Ruth.

Trailing them, Grace shelved her questions. But she found it wasn't quite as easy to dispel her thoughts.

Noah carried the few boxes up to the apartment easily. Ruth unpacked each, consulting with Grace before putting things away.

Grace remained strong throughout the process and Noah suspected the effort was for her aunt. As he had since meeting her, Noah admired Grace's uncomplaining nature. Sorrow had settled deeply in her eyes, but he wouldn't have expected less.

Even more admirable, she was always concerned

about others. Many of his patients ceased to think of anyone but themselves. Noah wondered if Grace realized how singularly astonishing that was.

"Ruth, you must be tired." Grace was looking at her aunt in concern. "You've fussed all day to make everything perfect."

"I'm fine," Ruth insisted. But fatigue had begun to set in the lines of her face.

"Okay, then. *I'm* tired." Grace smiled ruefully at her aunt. "Could we finish tomorrow?"

Ruth couldn't completely hide an expression of relief. "Of course, dear."

"I'll take the empty boxes down," Noah offered.

"That's kind of you," Ruth replied. "I think I'll go downstairs and make a pot of tea."

Noah glanced at the older woman, seeing her fatigue, guessing she would make another trip up the stairs with tea for Grace. "Ruth, is there a kettle in the kitchen here? And tea?"

"Yes, but—"

"I could bring you the tea…" Grace began.

Noah could see the frustration when Grace belatedly remembered she couldn't.

So he offered instead. "I can bring over a cup for you, Ruth. Give you and Grace both a chance to rest." He glanced between the two self-sufficient Stanton women, imagining each's mental tug-of-war.

"That would be nice," Ruth said finally. "I'm ready for my fuzzy slippers and an early night."

After her aunt left, Grace turned to him. "That was kind of you. Ruth doesn't often feel her age, but she's been overdoing it ever since my accident. I want to help...." She held up her hands. "But I'm useless."

He met her gaze. "Don't sell yourself short." Silently he marveled at the depth of her compassion in spite of her own injuries. "What you give Ruth can't be measured in physical terms."

Suddenly she looked vulnerable. As vulnerable as she had the day he'd first met her. "Do you really think so?"

"Absolutely."

"The lack of independence is one of the hardest things about my accident," she confessed. "I was accustomed to doing for myself and for others. It chafes me to stand by idly and ask for help."

"It's not a weakness, you know."

Her eyes widened, their color tonight taking on the hue of the surrounding blue walls. And again he glimpsed pleading. "But it is for me. It goes against my nature."

"Can't you accept it as a growing experience?" he asked quietly.

"That doesn't make any sense," Grace protested,

her lips trembling slightly. "How can it be an asset to become dependent?"

"There's a difference." Noah couldn't ignore the nudging of his faith. "Sometimes we have to ask for help in things greater than we are."

She grimaced, new pain marking the portion of her face that was exposed. "Perhaps *you* do."

"We all do."

Grace bent her head, then turned toward the open French doors. "It's not that black and white."

"You're right. That might be too easy. And faith is more complicated."

Her voice was both small and sad. "Yes, it is."

Noah wanted to probe further, but he could see the agitation in her tense muscles, the pain that was deeper than a physical one. So he crossed the room to the tiny kitchen. "Do you know where the tea bags are?"

"The cabinet over the sink."

The kettle was on the counter. After filling it with water, he put it on the stove. Between movements, he watched Grace as she continued to stand by the French doors. Her tawny blond hair was lit by a stream of moonlight. Her pose was quiet and still. And from his angle, no bandages were visible. She was lovely—a sculptor's vision. But cold marble couldn't do justice to her extraordinary warmth.

Nor could stone convey the depth of her incredibly changing eyes. Noah wondered what color they were right now. He was tempted to cross the room to see if her eyes would be silvery-gray, taking on the cast of the early moon.

The kettle whistled, startling them both.

Grace turned toward him. But Noah didn't see bandages. He still saw the same lovely vision. She was aptly named, he realized. She was full of grace.

Her gaze drifted from the screeching teakettle back toward him.

Seeing the questions forming in her expression, he turned to the counter and poured the hot water. "It should be ready soon."

"I'm glad Ruth's willing to have an early night. She'll appreciate the tea."

Noah put tea bags into the cups. "I'll take hers over now."

It didn't take long to deliver the tea and then return. "Ruth had already put on her fuzzy slippers," Noah reported, going to the kitchen.

He poured the mostly cooled tea from one mug into a small glass that Grace could get her fingers around. Picking up his own mug as well, he joined her on the small terrace. The fragrance of roses, touched by the day's sunshine, mingled with that of wild honeysuckle, drifting up and over the railing.

"It's so nice out here," she mused, her voice soft. "I miss the fresh air."

"I've told you to get all the fresh air you can tolerate."

"I know. But in the dark, no one can see me, judge me."

"You're so certain they would judge you in the light?"

She paused for a moment. "It's human nature. I've already seen the looks of pity. And curiosity. I've thought back on the times when I saw someone disfigured in some way. I remember the pity mostly. And I've always considered myself a fair-minded person. Still, it was there. Why should I expect any less from other people?"

"It seems you are expecting very little from people."

"I wonder if you'd say the same thing if we traded places."

"I've been very close to where you are," Noah reminded her quietly. "The scars my mother bears were shared by all of us."

Grace met his gaze. "I'm sorry. I didn't mean to minimize your mother's injuries. I suppose I thought they'd occurred so long ago that the memories might have dimmed. It was wrong of me to think so."

"It's natural. My mother's injuries did happen a long time ago. And it changed all of us in different ways. I have the luxury of the viewpoint of a surgeon, but no two people react exactly the same. My mother was consumed by guilt for the stress on the family, all the adjustments we had to make, but she remained strong. Some people become so despondent they never recover emotionally.''

She swallowed visibly. "Do you think I'll be one of those people, Noah?''

High above, the stars combined with the moon to illuminate the abbreviated terrace. And he knew he had to offer both gentleness and truth. "No. I think you are the exception, Grace. A true exception.''

She glanced up at him, her eyes revealing a touch of hope, and Noah wondered what he was doing. Grace was a patient and he had sworn it wouldn't happen again.

She turned away to quietly sip her tea, and Noah remembered.

It had been four years ago. Noah's life and ambitions were right on track. He had a prestigious position at one of the foremost hospitals in the country. He was making more money than he'd ever dreamed of and his social life was equally satisfying. His relationship with girlfriend Jordan Hall had grown serious. Although Jordan was high-strung, she had a magnetism he hadn't been able to ignore. It seemed everything he touched was charmed.

Then Jordan began a relentless campaign to have him perform cosmetic surgery on her face. Initially he hoped to dissuade her by telling the truth—that she was lovely as she was. Jordan wasn't convinced. Her superficiality aside, he told Jordan that he never worked on people he knew, and even if that wasn't so, he didn't perform frivolous operations. He worked only on major reconstructive jobs and birth defects. She continued to cajole him, but he remained firm. Then she told him she was going to another surgeon, one whom Noah knew to be inept.

Noah again tried to convince Jordan to change her mind. She also refused to consider any plastic surgeons Noah recommended. He was the best, she insisted, and she wanted him.

When she wouldn't be swayed, Noah reluctantly agreed to perform the operation. But to his horror, Jordan encountered unexpected complications. She had a heretofore undetected heart valve problem that would have come to light only with an echocardiogram, which wasn't one of the standard pre-op tests, especially for a young, apparently healthy young woman.

And despite his best efforts, Jordan died.

Noah remembered that agonizing time. Not only had she died, he had been responsible. Unable to shed the guilt, he had reevaluated his life, left behind his job and status. One thing he had carried with him—the resolve never to mix personal with professional.

Noah glanced at Grace, seeing the melancholy that had returned to her expression. She needed his help.

And he needed to stay far away from the temptation she presented.

Chapter Six

$\backsim$

But distance wasn't easy to maintain. Several weeks later, Grace had sunk deeper than ever into her self-imposed isolation. Noah was concerned that her failing optimism would be echoed in her recuperation. As was Ruth.

She had asked for his help again. The voice of the older woman—worried about Grace—had held repressed tears as she'd asked him to intervene.

Against his better judgment Noah had agreed. But luring Grace out wasn't easy. Speaking with Ruth, he learned some of Grace's hobbies. Her favorite was music—playing the piano.

Noah thought of the members of his band. It was a small group he had formed a few years earlier.

The four members were all friends, people he could trust.

The band member Noah specifically had in mind was Cindy Thompson Mallory. He felt she was the person most likely to draw out Grace, to ease her back into relating with other people. Hearing Grace's story, Cindy immediately agreed to help.

For the first attempt, Noah decided it was best to have only himself and Cindy. The entire band, even though small, might still be too much for Grace.

He had cajoled Grace into coming with him on the pretext that he needed a pianist. Although she protested she couldn't help with only one hand, he had insisted.

He had spoken of Cindy often while they had therapy. And when he told Grace that she would only have to meet Cindy, she finally capitulated.

Now, in the car, Noah glanced over at Grace, seeing her nervousness. "It's going to be okay."

She fiddled with her shirt, tugging again at the hem. "Sure."

But she didn't look sure at all. Now smoothing the fabric of her skirt, she watched out the window as the houses rolled by. "Like I've told you, Cindy's a good friend."

Grace's head bobbed uncertainly.

"I met her when I needed a friend," Noah confided, not sure where the admission came from.

"After I left Houston I was trying to find out just where I fit in again."

Grace finally pulled her gaze away from the disappearing landscape. "That's hard to believe."

He angled his head in her direction. "Oh?"

"You seem very certain of yourself."

Noah considered that. "It's a good cover. But I wouldn't recommend adopting it."

Her head dipped downward. "I doubt any cover will work for me."

He hated the discouragement in her voice. "The bandages won't last forever."

"In some ways I wish they would."

Noah knew that many patients hated the thought of their residual scarring being exposed. He glanced again at Grace. Although only half her face was visible, it was consumed by emotion. He suspected tears were only a breath away and knew she needed a distraction. "How old were you when you began to play the piano?"

She was quiet for a moment. "Five. My mother taught me." Grace laughed softly. "She was as insistent as you are that I stretch my hands."

Noah watched as the memory played over her face. "Smart woman."

"Hmpf." But her lips twitched.

Slowing down, Noah turned into the church parking lot.

Grace squealed. "What are we doing here?"

"This is where the band practices—in the rec hall."

"That's the only reason?" she asked suspiciously, studying the graceful architectural design of the church.

"No hidden motives." He placed one hand on his chest. "Cross my heart."

Grace suspected that Noah hoped some of the sacred ambience the church radiated would rub off on her. But she knew it wasn't that easy.

However, once inside, she felt a rush of memories. Deep in her past she had felt welcome in church. Not anymore.

They walked down the hall toward a small room, and to her relief they didn't meet anyone on the way.

Still she was nervous. "Are there any other people here today?"

"Shouldn't be. The pastor's office is in her home. She has a growing family, so it's easier for her to work there."

"Her?" Grace questioned in surprise.

"Yes. Katherine Carlson. She is our first female minister—one of the best decisions we ever made."

She had scarcely absorbed that when a woman approached them. Grace had a startling impression of red hair and vivacity.

"Hello," the woman greeted her. "I'm Cindy Mallory. It's a pleasure to meet you."

"I've heard a lot about you," Grace managed, the words coming more easily than she expected.

"Yipes," Cindy replied with a wry but warm smile. "That's scary. And yet you came anyway."

Grace found herself relaxing a fraction. "It was all good."

"Noah's too kind," Cindy replied, her warmth compelling.

"I've heard about your triplets." Grace had loved Noah's tales of the precocious girls.

Cindy's face softened. "I shouldn't brag, but they're wonderful children. I'm constantly amazed by their imagination and whimsy. And even though they look nearly alike, they're very different. Especially as they're getting older. Such individual personalities that at times it's hard to believe they're triplets. And don't even get me started on my oldest son. He's the smartest boy in his class, and the baby…" Her voice filled with chagrin. "I'm sorry, I'm going on and on about them."

"I enjoyed it." No longer certain children were in her future, Grace liked hearing the tales of the triplets.

"You're sweet to say so. I know I babble endlessly about the children. My husband just rolls his eyes. It's okay if you do, too."

Grace was surprised but not overwhelmed by Cindy's exuberant personality. "What if I withhold judgment?"

Cindy grinned. "Spoken like a woman after my own heart. I'm glad you're able to sit in on the practice today. Usually I'm stuck with the guys."

"Thanks," Noah responded, sounding properly insulted.

But Cindy didn't seem particularly concerned. "Pooh. You know that you men talk about sports and cars and other equally fascinating subjects."

Grace stiffened. "Will they be here today?"

"Just Cindy and me today," Noah replied.

"I need the extra practice," Cindy explained. "My family takes up so much time that I haven't learned my lyrics." She cocked her head. "Do you sing?"

Grace fumbled with a reply. "Not in your league."

"I asked because sometimes I can't make a performance and Noah could use another singer." Cindy didn't wait for a reply, turning to Noah. "Which reminds me. I can't perform next week. My Rainbow class has a special activity." She turned back to Grace. "The Rainbow class is a pet project of mine. I started it a few years ago for children who need a little extra attention, and it's grown considerably."

"And you love it," Grace guessed.

Cindy's smile softened again. "Absolutely."

Grace could see why Noah had chosen this particular woman as the first person for her to meet in Rosewood. Cindy was warm, open and accepting. A bit more of her tension subsided.

Cindy picked up some pages of music. "Noah told me you play the piano."

Grace swallowed, feeling the weight of her injuries. "I used to."

Cindy didn't look surprised, nor did she give Grace that pitying glance she'd become accustomed to. "Do you think you could pick out the melody line with your left hand?"

"I don't really know." Grace tentatively stretched her fingers. "This hand *is* getting better." She speculated for a moment, then came to a decision. "Why don't I try?"

Cindy and Noah both grinned.

"Don't expect too much," she warned them, walking to the piano. She settled on the bench, then tentatively ran the fingers of her left hand over first the smooth, dark wood, then the keys.

As she picked out the notes of a familiar song, Grace felt a small spurt of her old confidence. Neither Noah or Cindy commented and Grace was glad they didn't feel compelled to cheer her on. She couldn't take any overly inflated rah-rahs.

When Grace finished, Cindy placed a sheet of music on the piano. "Could we try this one? You could play through it before I sing."

Grace nodded. Luckily it was an easy piece. The second time, Cindy added her voice. And Noah came in with his guitar. By the following verse, Grace found herself humming.

Humming, she realized with a start.

It was hard to imagine.

"I think that was pretty darn good for the first time we've practiced together," Cindy declared. She shuffled through the music, lifting out another sheet. "Why don't we run through this one, as well?"

Noah's beeper went off just as Grace accepted the music. He glanced at the digital readout. "I'm sorry, ladies. I have to run to the E.R." He glanced at Grace, then Cindy. "If Grace doesn't mind, could you give her a ride home?"

"Sure," Cindy replied, looking at Grace.

Relieved that she already felt comfortable with Cindy, Grace nodded. "Fine with me if it doesn't take Cindy out of her way."

"Thanks. Sorry to cut this short." Noah replaced his beeper, then sprinted toward the exit.

"Ah, the life of a doctor," Cindy said with a sigh. "The band has learned to be very, very flexible."

"He doesn't seem to mind the interruptions. But

then, I haven't known him nearly as long as you have."

"Noah's a rare and special man."

Grace glanced up at her curiously.

Cindy read the silent question. "No. I was never involved with him. When I met Noah, my heart was already taken."

"Your husband?"

Cindy nodded. "Although he wasn't my husband at the time. Now, there's a story." She paused. "Maybe we could have some lunch, get to know each other."

Grace felt regret laced with panic. "I don't go out."

Cindy wasn't fazed. "We could pick up a pizza and take it home, if you're game."

Unused to fielding social situations in her new condition, Grace hesitated.

"I really am a bull in a china shop," Cindy continued. "If you're tired, I don't mean to press."

It had been a big day for her, agreeing to meet Cindy, entering the church—both had been taxing. But Grace didn't want to turn into a fragile butterfly afraid to even eat lunch with a new acquaintance. "Actually, lunch sounds nice."

Cindy smiled widely. "Great. Now, for the big decision…"

Grace smiled, as well. "Pepperoni or cheese?"

By the time they were on their second slice of pizza, Grace felt she had known Cindy for years.

Also a woman without pretense, Cindy was easy to talk to, honest and refreshingly frank. She neither dwelled on Grace's injuries nor pretended they didn't exist.

While Grace had invited her aunt to join them, Cindy had casually gone about setting the table. Ruth had declined, suggesting the "girls" should have some time on their own.

Cindy didn't pepper her with questions. Instead she told Grace about her husband, Flynn Mallory, how she loved his three daughters as her own, and how they'd come to adopt their son.

"Your husband sounds like a very special man," Grace observed.

Cindy's expression grew reflective. "He is. We had impossible circumstances to overcome, but with the Lord's help..." She paused, then smiled ruefully. "You don't want to hear all this!"

"Actually I do," Grace protested. "Unless it's too personal."

"No, not anymore."

"It used to be?"

"When I loved him from afar, so to speak, I only told my best friend, Katherine. It was too painful to share with anyone else."

Grace studied the other woman. "I realize I've

just met you, but you don't strike me as the shy type.''

Cindy laughed. ''I see you've read me perfectly. No, I'm not shy, but Flynn was married to my sister. We both met him at the same time. I fell hard. He did, too, but in Julia's direction. So I moved here to Rosewood.''

''It must have been a difficult situation for you.''

Cindy nodded. ''I loved Julia with all my heart and I wanted her to be happy. She and Flynn had each other and the triplets. Their life seemed picture-perfect.''

''And?'' Grace questioned quietly.

''Julia died.'' Cindy swallowed, sadness flashing in her eyes.

''I'm sorry.''

Cindy acknowledged the sympathy with a shake of her head. ''Even though I could never love another man the way I loved Flynn, I would never have chosen to lose my sister in order to have him.''

''Of course not!'' Grace's intuition told her that Cindy had a good heart.

The leap of faith was rewarded with a huge smile. ''It helps me to know that I can raise Julia's girls the way she would have wanted.''

''I think it takes a special person to do that and to adopt another child.''

"Funny," Cindy mused. "I never think of myself as special, just lucky."

"Which is probably why you're special."

Cindy smiled again. "I definitely see potential in this friendship!"

Grace smiled as well, thinking how refreshingly normal their lunch had been. No talk of injuries or the accident.

And Grace read the genuine regret in Cindy's expression when she glanced at her watch.

"I can't believe it's so late! Flynn will be worried if I'm not home soon. He's great about watching the kids, but I don't like to take advantage of him."

"I understand completely."

"Let's do this again soon, okay?" Cindy picked up her purse. "You're so easy to talk to I feel like I've known you forever."

Grace was surprised at how much she'd enjoyed the day. "I feel that way, too."

"We can probably reschedule another band practice for later this week. Would that work for you?"

Thinking of her empty days, broken up only by medical appointments and therapy, Grace nodded. "I think so."

"I'll talk to Noah and call you," Cindy said with a wave.

Noah. Grace had him to thank for persisting until she agreed to meet Cindy. She remembered the other woman's words about him. A rare and exceptional man. Perhaps, but he was still a man. The growing accolades simply made her more suspicious. Noah was beginning to sound too good to be true.

By evening Grace was tired. But in a good way, she thought.

"So, it was a fun day?" Ruth asked, handing Grace a dessert plate.

Grace eyed the cheesecake with an interest she hadn't felt in months. "Yes. And it surprised me."

"Ah. Couldn't foresee that?" Ruth asked sagely.

"I'm not *trying* to be difficult," Grace reminded her.

"No one said you were." Ruth examined her piece of cheesecake critically. "Think this stacks up to the big-city variety?"

Grace took a bite. "It's delicious! I doubt there's better cheesecake in all of New York."

Ruth smiled. "After the final surgery, we'll have to go there and find out."

Grace felt the lump in her throat thicken. "I doubt there's much traveling in my future."

"Pish. I've been waiting all my life to visit New York City. If I can handle the journey, so can you."

"You know it's not the traveling," Grace replied, voice tight.

"Gracie, every day is going to bring more healing. Yesterday you wouldn't have believed meeting Cindy would be fun."

"I suppose. But that's a far cry from traveling."

Ruth carved a second small slice of cake. "One step at a time, dear."

Grace couldn't imagine such a day.

But before she could comment, the phone rang.

"Would you get that, Gracie?" Ruth held up cheesecake-covered fingers.

Expecting one of Ruth's many friends, Grace was startled to hear Patrick's voice.

"Grace? Is that you?"

She couldn't speak.

"Grace? I thought Ruth would answer."

She cleared her throat, fighting the rush of emotions. She had hoped to hear from him, despaired of ever hearing from him, had imagined her own scathing response should he dare. But now only silence echoed over the wires.

"Grace? I...I'm not sure what to say...."

"Why are you calling, Patrick?"

He seemed stunned by the blunt question. After seconds of silence, his voice was hesitant. "I want to see how you're doing."

"You don't really want to *see* me, do you, Patrick?"

"Grace, it's a bad choice of words. I want to know how you're doing, if you're feeling okay."

"Okay?" The ludicrous choice of words rocked her. "Okay is for a day that's not great, or food that's good, even if it's not your favorite. *Okay* does not apply to a person who's been disfigured beyond repair."

Patrick stuttered for a few moments. But Grace didn't feel any pity for his discomfort.

"Obviously I've called at a bad time." In control of his voice again, Patrick seemed determined to control the call as well. "So I'll say good-night."

"Goodbye."

The click of his phone disconnecting sounded unnaturally loud.

Grace replaced the receiver and turned around. The knowing look on Ruth's face reinforced the discomfort of the call.

"You didn't give him much of a chance," Ruth observed.

"More of a chance than he gave me." New hurt sliced over the old. "He didn't even intend to talk to me. It was a duty call so he can report back to our friends and not look as though he's run away."

"But your friends—"

"Bad choice of words, Ruth. Our social circle is made up of associates, people we networked with. Patrick has an image to maintain."

Ruth hesitated. "Have you spoken to any of them since you've been out of the hospital?"

"No. They sent obligatory flower arrangements, but that's as personal as it will get." Grace reflected on the people she had surrounded herself with in the city. Close friendships from her younger days had withered from lack of care. People moved on and away.

"I'm blessed to have friends in my church, ones I can count on for anything," Ruth commented.

"I'm happy for you," Grace replied tactfully. She didn't need any more hints right now about seeking out the church. Patrick's call only reinforced her feelings. The Lord had turned His back on her again.

Nearly a week later, Grace had a call of another sort. Noah and Cindy needed her for another practice. She and Cindy had spoken several times since they'd met. The fledgling friendship reminded Grace of a time, years earlier, when she'd spent more time with friends than in concentrating on her career. She hadn't thought it was something she missed, but now she wondered.

The pace in Rosewood seemed to allow for more introspection. Grace realized that she had excess time because she wasn't working, but it was more than that. Every hour of every day in Houston had been packed, brimming with activity.

Now, as she watched out the window, Grace wondered if this was simply part of healing, these different feelings about things once familiar. She would ask Noah.

Expecting him any minute now for what he called a new approach to therapy, she also wondered if it was normal for her to look forward so much to seeing her doctor.

And that she couldn't ask Noah.

The Porsche turned in to the driveway, its sleek lines gleaming in the late-afternoon sun. The sun also lit Noah's dark, thick hair. There was both energy and strength in his movements. It struck her again that it was hard to believe he was still unattached.

Walking to the door, she opened it just moments after he knocked.

"Well, hello," he greeted her, clearly surprised by the speed of her response.

"I saw you coming up the walk," she explained. This man had seen her worst scars, yet she didn't want him to know how much she enjoyed watching him.

"Am I late?"

"No. I'm early."

He didn't question her response. "Then I take it you're ready?"

Grace swallowed, hoping she wasn't making a mistake. "I think so."

Noah had been asking her to come to the church

to practice on the organ, believing it would be good for her more damaged hand. Having kept at the exercises he imposed, she was beginning to have some slight movement in her right hand.

And he had convinced her that this was another step in her therapy. In a weak moment, she told herself.

Because she hadn't intended to go back to the Rosewood Community Church, despite encouragement from Noah, Ruth and now Cindy. But it had been difficult to argue against Noah's reasoning.

As they drove through town, Grace marveled at all the people who recognized Noah and waved to him. "I think you could run for mayor and win."

He laughed. "A doctor in a town this size is well-known. Occupational hazard."

"And the Porsche is hard to miss."

"Don't I know it. But it was impossible to turn down."

She turned to stare at him. "You mean it was a gift?"

"From a grateful patient. I refused at first—told him to donate the money to the Rosewood Medical Foundation. He said he'd donate twice the value of the Porsche, provided I accepted the car as well. The foundation was in its beginning stages and I couldn't say no."

She studied him. "That's a big tribute to your work."

"I was only doing my job, which I tried to explain to him. But when it comes to people's children, emotions overrule logic."

"You operated on his child?"

"Yes. His daughter was burned in a camping accident and he was distraught."

"But you were able to help her?"

Noah glanced over at her. "Yes. And the child has a bright future."

Grace cleared her throat. "Is that a pep talk?"

"*You* asked about the Porsche."

"So I did." She paused. "And maybe I do need a pep talk today."

"Which is bothering you more—therapy on that hand, or going to the church?"

"Everything has been so jumbled since the accident—it's difficult to sort out a lot of things."

"I can understand that."

"You have a unique perspective, having been on both sides of this—patient's family and physician."

"My mother's accident impacted me a lot. Not only did it guide my career, it taught me what was valuable."

Grace remained quiet for the next few minutes as they completed the short drive to the church. Once out of the car, Noah didn't turn toward the rec hall.

Instead he walked to the doors of the sanctuary. Taking out a key, he put it in the lock.

Grace watched in surprise.

He caught the question in her eyes. "I have a key because I'm the music director. And I work with the youth, through the music program, so the key comes in handy."

She realized he was more than a simple churchgoer. He was clearly committed to the church despite his already crowded schedule. "You enjoy it, don't you?"

"Yes. You know how I feel about music. And the kids are a bonus."

"Does that come from having a large family? Liking kids, I mean."

"I suppose so. I just hate the thought of a kid failing or not reaching his potential because no one took an interest in him."

Never having known a man like him, Grace was overwhelmed by his sense of honor.

When she didn't speak, he took her elbow, leading her inside. The sanctuary was quiet, dimly lit. But as she glanced farther inside, she saw sunlight flowing in from the stained glass windows, the bright beams piercing the interior, glancing over the pews.

They walked up the wide center aisle and Grace felt a bittersweet rush of feeling. She could see her mother's smiling face, then the pain on her father's. It was a sense of homecoming, yet a sense of betrayal. Confused, she followed Noah up the steps to the organ.

He gestured to the bench. Hesitantly she sat down. When Noah joined her, she felt immediate relief. It occurred to her that the physical pain of this new therapy might fall far short of the emotional distress.

He leafed through the music, put one piece on top and quietly began to play. The artistry he demonstrated in the operating room spun from his fingers, his song filling the empty room.

Grace closed her eyes against the emotion the notes evoked. Beneath his hands, the music spoke of beauty. It reached out to her, touched her. Swallowing against the sudden lump in her throat, Grace acknowledged how much she missed the tactile feel of the piano keys, the beauty of the notes.

Finishing the piece, Noah took her hand. She would have resisted the gesture, but knew he was acting only as her doctor. The formerly massive bandages had been reduced so that the fingers of her right hand were now fully exposed. They were stiff and unresponsive, but that didn't deter him.

He put her through the warm-up exercises they had been doing. Then Noah stretched out her fingers, gently placing them on the keys. When they didn't respond, he covered them with his own larger fingers, pressing on them gently.

Grace bit her lips. She was used to the pain of stretching her hand, but this wasn't the same.

Aware of his touch in a different way, she held her breath as he carefully moved her hand in unison with his. It was as though they held hands. And, to her surprise, her skin tingled beneath his. Of course it did, she told herself. After all, it had been months since she'd held a man's hand.

Intensely aware of her terribly flawed appearance, Grace swallowed, hoping her feelings would subside. Afraid to look at him, she stared instead at the organ keys, quiet pressing around her.

A sudden noise in the back of the church made them both look up at the same time.

A teenaged boy hurried up the aisle. "Noah?" The boy didn't stop, charging toward them.

Grace shrank back as Noah rose.

"Robert?" Noah questioned as he walked down the steps. "What is it?"

"Your office said you might be here." The boy was breathless, perspiring.

"Take a breath. What's wrong?"

Making certain she couldn't be seen, Grace peeked around the organ, seeing the teenager's distress.

Robert's breathing slowed as he held out a wrinkled piece of paper. "The scores on my college admission tests."

Noah accepted the letter. "You're a junior. You'll have another chance to take them."

"My English scores aren't going to get better if I take the test a dozen times, Noah." The boy's voice dulled with discouragement. "And if I blow the test I won't get my scholarship."

"There are no problems without answers, Robert. You know that."

Robert shook his head. "If I don't get the scholarship, I won't be able to go to college."

"Then we'll have to find you an English tutor."

"You know my dad got laid off. There's no money for a tutor. I give the pay from my summer job to my mom to help out. It's what I want to do, but still that doesn't leave any extra."

Noah placed an arm over the boy's shoulders. "Robert, I promise we'll work this out. I wish I were better at English. Science was my strong suit. We'll think of something, though."

"I never thought about what I'd do if I didn't get to go to college," Robert said in a defeated voice.

Grace felt her heart go out to the young man. Although she had been on her own when only a few years older, the sale of her parents' home had left her enough money to attend college without worry.

She watched Robert as he confided in Noah. The

boy should be rewarded for working to help his family, not penalized for their situation.

She admired Noah's deft handling of the boy. Clearly he had a good relationship with the youth for Robert to show such trust in him.

It was a shame that Robert was having trouble with English. That had been her best subject in school.

An idea crashed into her thoughts. *She could help the young man.* And money wouldn't be an issue.

But could she handle it?

Grace was quiet as they finished the day's therapy, distracted by thoughts of the defeated-looking teenager.

As they drove the short distance to her home, Grace kept imagining how it would have felt to be in the boy's shoes, to doubt you even had a future.

"You're awfully quiet," Noah commented.

"Just thinking about Robert. That's a big burden for someone so young."

"He's resourceful."

"He shouldn't have to be. He should be enjoying this time. It's supposed to be carefree, not fraught with worry over whether he has a future." Her mind made up, she turned in her seat. "Noah, I could tutor Robert."

Stopped at a traffic light, he looked over at her in surprise. "You?"

"I'm no teacher, but English was my minor."

He studied her. "I'm just surprised."

"I guess I am, too." Grace knew she might have given up on herself, but not on others. Especially the young man.

"Robert's a good kid. His family's had a rough time, but he's still concentrating on his grades. With the right schooling, I think he'll make a lot of his future."

"Then we'll have to make sure that happens," Grace said with a confidence she didn't feel.

Meeting Noah's gaze, she glimpsed the approval in his eyes.

And was terrified to realize how much that mattered.

Chapter Seven

Grace was nervous. Noah had driven Robert to her apartment, introduced him and stayed for a short while. But now as she closed the door behind Noah, Grace felt unsure of herself.

"Miss Stanton?"

She turned toward the boy.

"Yes, Robert?"

"Well, before we started, I just wanted to say something...."

Grace braced herself.

"It's really great of you to help me. Noah told me about your high-profile career, how accomplished you are. And I want you to know I won't disappoint you."

"Of course you won't," she replied in a rush of relief.

"And I'm going to pay you."

"I don't want your money, Robert. It's my pleasure to help you."

"If you won't take money, then I'll work it off," he insisted.

Seeing the pride in his eyes, she wavered. "I don't have a lot of work that needs to be done. But my aunt Ruth could probably use a hand with her yard."

His eyes lit up. "Sure."

She couldn't prevent a smile at his enthusiasm. "Then I guess we'd better get started. Let's sit at the table."

He followed her instructions and she was relieved that he wasn't staring at her. When they had first been introduced, she'd seen the look in his eyes that struck most people when they saw her extensive bandages. But she guessed that Noah had briefed him, because Robert didn't ask any questions.

As Noah had told her, Robert was extremely bright. And he was a diligent student. But she could see that he would need quite a bit of instruction. His strengths were in science and math. She couldn't help wondering if a lack of interest had caused the deficiency in his literary knowledge.

So she talked to him about his other interests,

hoping that she could think of a way to tie them in to the classics he needed to conquer. And Grace found herself relaxing and enjoying the chat.

There was a quiet knock on the door. Grace glanced at the clock, surprised to see how much time had passed.

The door opened and Ruth peered around the edge. "Am I interrupting?"

"Not at all. We're finished for today."

Ruth walked inside. "Great. I brought cookies."

"Umm. Chocolate chip." Grace turned to Robert. "She makes the best cookies in the world. I have milk and soda. Which do you want with your cookies?"

He decided quickly. "Milk."

"The only drink for cookies," Ruth agreed, taking the milk from the refrigerator and filling three glasses.

"Living next door to my aunt is like having a twenty-four-hour restaurant and bakery on the premises," Grace confided as she reached for a cookie.

Grinning, Robert took another cookie when Ruth held out the plate. "Thanks."

Companionably they munched on the cookies.

Robert drained his glass, then reached for his notebook. "I'd better be going."

Grace thought of his struggling family and made her voice casual. "Robert, could you do us a favor and take the rest of the cookies? We're watching our calories and if the cookies are around we'll blow our diets."

Robert seemed to accept her story at face value. "Sure. They're awesome cookies."

After he left, Ruth met Grace's gaze. "He's a nice boy."

"Yes, he is."

"And it looks as though your tutoring went well."

Grace smiled. "I think so. And thanks for picking up on the cookie story."

Ruth shrugged. "You told me about his family. We have enough, and I like to share what the Lord's blessed me with."

Grace sipped her milk, avoiding a reply.

That didn't deter Ruth. "I had a phone call from Patrick."

"Hmm."

"He didn't have the phone number to your apartment. I had a convenient attack of old age and couldn't place your number. Want to tell me what's going on?"

Grace fiddled with the paper napkin. "I didn't think you'd need one after the demonstration the other night."

"I have been wondering why he hasn't been to visit since you've come to Rosewood."

"I wondered about that for about two weeks, then

the answer was pretty clear. Remember, he had dozens of excuses while I was in the hospital in Houston.''

Ruth frowned. "I assumed you discouraged him from visiting."

"Somewhat. But wouldn't you think he'd come anyway?"

Ruth's face revealed her opinion, even though she didn't voice it.

So Grace pressed. "I see you've got an opinion. Out with it."

"It doesn't matter what I think. This is your life, Grace. I can fuss and hover and love you to pieces, but I can't determine what's in your heart. I will say that I think you deserve a man who's strong...as strong as you are."

Grace looked at her aunt in surprise. "You think I'm strong?"

"Of course you are. You always have been."

Grace thought of the fear and uncertainty that had become her life. "I'm not so sure."

"It's taken a great deal of courage to come this far. Early in your life you faced great loss and stayed strong. You've survived injuries that would have killed most people. And it took strength to offer to tutor young Robert."

Grace started to protest.

Ruth waved away the words. "You risked rejec-

tion and that always requires courage, my dear.''
She paused. ''I think the Lord is closer than you're
ready to acknowledge. Because He gives us courage.''

Looking down at the well-polished table, Grace
saw her distorted reflection. Closing her eyes, she
thought of all the loss. Her mother, her father...now
her life and career as she had known them. And
Patrick.

Funny, if their situations had been reversed, she
would have glued herself to his side. She'd thought
she had tested him in all the ways that had mattered
before she had agreed to marry him.

Perhaps there was no man capable of sticking by
through such a horrendous accident. A picture of
Noah flashed through her thoughts. But that wasn't
a fair comparison. He was her doctor. If he'd been
in her life simply as a man, he probably would have
run as quickly as Patrick had.

Ruth's voice was gentle. ''What should I tell Patrick if he calls back?''

Grace looked at her ruined hands. ''I doubt it mat-
ters.'' And though she was able to utter the words
in a matter-of-fact voice, the hurt still sliced through
her.

How could he have claimed to love her, then deserted her?

It was evident to Grace that Cindy and Katherine
were good and close friends. Their rapport was easy,

natural. Yet Grace was still nervous, meeting yet another stranger.

"Isn't this house fabulous?" Katherine was asking. "Cindy decorated it before she and Flynn decided to get married."

The comment intrigued Grace. She guessed it was meant to. "It's amazing that she knew his tastes so well."

Cindy placed an interesting-looking salad on the table. "It was his way of letting me know he appreciated me for myself, not as a substitute for my sister."

Even though Cindy sounded matter-of-fact, Grace hesitated.

Cindy noticed and smiled. "It's all right. I know the road to our marriage was unusual, to say the least."

"We both chose the hard way," Katherine added.

Grace wondered at Katherine's story, almost as much as she wondered about the fact that she was a female minister. "But you're happy now?"

"Ecstatic," Katherine replied. "And I know how lucky I am."

"Good men are hard to find," Grace agreed, unable to keep all the bitterness from her voice. Immediately she regretted it, not wanting to put a damper on the luncheon Cindy had planned. "Sorry. I'm off men at the moment."

"I've been there," Cindy said, offering a basket of rolls. "And I didn't have any easy answers, either."

Grace looked at the faces of the two concerned women. Faces that were whole, lovely. She appreciated their overtures of friendship, but neither could understand how she felt. She pushed the salad around on her plate, noticing the sunflower seeds and dried cranberries. But she had no appetite.

Katherine and Cindy exchanged an anxious glance.

"I know we can't truly understand what you're going through," Katherine said. "We haven't walked in your shoes, so to speak. But we want to understand, to offer our support."

"That's incredibly kind of you," Grace replied, unable to tamp down the mountain of sadness welling inside.

"It's an occupational hazard," Katherine replied, her eyes filled with concern.

"I don't need a minister," Grace replied. "I appreciate the offer, but—"

"How about a friend?" Katherine interjected.

"Me, too," Cindy added.

Grace felt her throat thicken. "You're both being so wonderful."

"Nothing of the sort!" Cindy objected. "Friends are the treasures of life."

"Absolutely," Katherine chimed in.

"I'm overwhelmed."

"Good. In that case, we can draft you to help with the Rainbow class." Cindy raised her eyebrows to punctuate the remark.

Panic replaced gratitude. "I don't think—"

"Children are very accepting," Katherine told her gently. "But don't let Cindy bully you into helping before you're ready."

"Me? Bully?" Cindy eyed them with mock outrage. "Would I do that?"

Katherine laughed. "When our church was nearly destroyed by fire, Cindy was climbing all over the scaffolding and dragging along anyone she could find to help. Don't fall for that innocent look of hers."

Some of Grace's tension subsided. "I'll remember that."

Cindy groaned. "Katherine, how can I muster volunteers with you around?"

"Oh, I'm quite sure you'll manage," Katherine replied tartly.

Cindy rolled her eyes. "See what I have to put up with?"

"I imagine you hold your own," Grace replied.

Katherine and Cindy both chuckled. And Grace relaxed a fraction more.

Cindy refilled the glasses with a special limeade. "You'll have to meet our husbands."

"Another time," Katherine added. "And the kids, if you want to brave them. We've got quite a tribe between us."

"I'm not sure I'm ready to meet that many new people."

Katherine clucked sympathetically. "Sorry. Our enthusiasm sometimes outruns our good sense. Let's just enjoy today. Tomorrow will sort itself out." She picked up a roll. "Do you know Cindy makes these from sprouted wheat? They're good in spite of that."

Grace swallowed. She was grateful that they were smoothing over things. But it drove home the starkness of the truth.

Her life would never, ever be the same.

It had been a long day. After lunch, the women had talked, exclaimed over the newest photos of the children and whiled the hours away.

Exhausted, Grace wanted to do nothing but crawl under a comforter and relax in front of an old movie. But she knew Ruth would be expecting a report on the visit.

Taking the back way, Grace entered through the

kitchen. Seeing it was empty, she pushed open the swinging door to the living room.

And stopped straightaway.

Patrick sat on the couch beside Ruth.

Seeing Grace, he rose.

Ruth's words trailed off as she, too, caught sight of her niece.

"Grace, we were just talking about you," Patrick greeted her.

"I bet."

He looked shocked by her abrupt response.

Ruth's face filled with concern. "Grace, I'm sure you're tired after your long day."

Patrick didn't take the hint. "We have a lot to talk about, don't we, Grace?"

"Do we?"

The smile on his handsome face stretched thin. "Are you going to answer every question with a question?"

"Does that bother you?" she asked perversely.

"I haven't heard about the progress you've made yet." He angled his head, studying her. "You have fewer bandages than I thought you would."

Immediately self-conscious, she lost her edge. "Oh."

"Her surgeries have gone well so far," Ruth interjected.

Patrick's gaze wandered over Grace. "You've already had some plastic surgery?"

Grace winced beneath the layers of gauze. All of the pain she'd gone through since the accident focused into one sharp jabbing wave.

"Grace doesn't like to talk about the procedures," Ruth said hastily.

"Oh...sorry." Patrick looked first at Ruth, then at Grace. "I figured you'd be used to it by now."

Grace found her voice. "I'm not sure that ever happens."

"We can talk about it over dinner," Patrick replied. "Surely there's a restaurant open, even in Rosewood."

Staring at him, Grace wondered how he could be so completely clueless. As though she could possibly feel comfortable in such a situation. "It probably wouldn't be up to your standards."

"Probably not," he replied with a smile. "But I can rough it for one evening."

"I already have dinner started," Ruth intervened. "Why don't you stay and join us?"

Grace wasn't sure whether to thank or strangle her aunt.

Patrick glanced at his watch. "I can't stay too long. I have an early meeting in the morning."

It hadn't occurred to Grace that Patrick would have driven all the way from Houston for such a short visit. "Ruth, perhaps Patrick and I can talk now. Then he can get back on the road sooner."

Ruth, always a gracious hostess, rose. "I'll be in the kitchen if you need me."

The quiet swish of the door swinging closed behind Ruth was the only sound for a few moments.

"So, what brings you here, Patrick?"

"You, of course."

"Of course?" She angled her head so that the bandaged side was farther away from him. "I don't think that's a given. Certainly not after all this time."

"I was afraid that might be a sticking point," he replied ruefully, his boyish grin urging her to forgive what he considered a mild trespass.

"A sticking point? You weren't even certain I would survive when you walked away. And since then…" Raw pain choked off her voice.

"Look, I'm sorry, Grace. It was a foolish, cowardly thing to do. But I'd never had any experience with sick people."

"I wasn't *sick*. I was injured, nearly killed. It's not quite the same thing as having a tiff that can be patched up with flowers or chocolates."

He frowned. "You sound as though you don't *want* to patch up things."

Her caustic laugh was laced with pain. "That's convenient for you, isn't it? Lay the blame on me.

You walk away unscathed, able to tell everyone how you tried and how unreasonable I was.''

"Clearly you're not thinking straight. Perhaps I should come back when you're feeling better.''

"That may not happen.''

Patrick stood up. "I'll call you.''

She couldn't reply without lashing out, so she remained quiet.

He walked to the front hall, then turned back for a moment. "Goodbye, Grace.''

"Goodbye.'' It was all she could manage, and even that single word was an incredible effort.

As she watched him through the window, she saw that he checked his watch as he walked to his car. She guessed his mind had already skipped ahead to his next obligation.

That's all she was to him anymore. An obligation. An uncooperative one, at that.

Chapter Eight

Nearly two weeks later, Noah stood at the barbecue pit in his backyard, gazing at the hot coals. Friends were starting to filter through the gate, and the low rumble of conversation scattered around him.

He hadn't invited too many people. The members of his band, friends from church and his family. Then, on an impulse, he'd invited Grace and her aunt.

Although he had intended to broaden the distance between them, he was worried about Grace. Her depression was a visible thing and Ruth had again asked for his help. He hadn't been able to refuse.

He thought Grace would be comfortable at the barbecue. She had met everyone he had invited except for his family. The open acceptance she'd received from Cindy, Katherine, Robert and the members of his band had given her the courage to risk meeting a few people.

When his friends had heard about Grace's unfortunate accident, each had been eager to help her ease into new situations and become a part of the community. Cindy and Katherine had convinced her to meet their families, and she had done well on those outings.

Still, he knew Grace was anxious. This would be her first group situation. He didn't count the numerous times she went to his office or the hospital. There she was in the company of other injured or ill people.

Noah had told Grace that he had also invited his family. When she balked, he reminded her of his mother's accident. His family had heard about Grace and wanted to meet her.

His mother, in particular, had felt an instant empathy with Grace when she'd heard her story. But all of his family was sensitive to the injuries Grace had received.

Even though her anxiety was visible, Grace reluctantly agreed that she would meet them, as well.

Leaving the grill, Noah checked the long table he had set up on the rear deck to hold the food. Everyone would bring a dish—salads, baked beans and desserts. His specialty was barbecuing brisket, a long, slow process that made the meat tender and succulent.

He reached for a few more folding outdoor chairs to add to the ones he had already set up in the yard. The large lawn was one of the many things he liked about his nineteenth-century home. The generous grassy area was only a portion of the acreage that had come with the house. There was still plenty of land in slowly growing Rosewood, so there wasn't a rush to reduce yards to the postage-stamp size often found in larger cities.

For the most part, Noah had kept the integrity of the original house. He liked the faded brick, the tall, distinctive gables and the charm only age could provide.

He had added the wide, long wraparound deck,to the rear of the house, but he hadn't sacrificed any of the tall, aged trees that provided enough shade to cool the hottest Texas days. They, along with decades-old rosebushes and gardenias, defined the large space, making it cozy, inviting.

Glancing around the yard, Noah realized he had made more preparations for this barbecue than any social event he could remember.

This fact should have made him reconsider the gathering. He knew better than to invest his emotions in a patient.

Hearing a noise at the side gate, Noah walked

across the yard and saw the object of his thoughts. "Grace, welcome."

She smiled, glancing around anxiously. "Hi."

Ruth was only a few steps behind. "Noah, I can smell that brisket a block away!"

Having always liked this spunky, caring woman, he found it easy to joke with her. "Meets with your approval, then?"

"You cooked the beef slow, didn't you?"

He grinned. "Yes, ma'am."

"I may never leave, then," she declared, walking toward the brick pit at the other side of the yard.

Grace glanced around nervously. "Is your family here?"

He took her elbow. "They should be here any time now. My family's really looking forward to meeting you."

He could see her swallow. "Me, too."

"It's all right to be nervous. But you'll see how easy they are to be with."

"It's still so difficult...." She paused. "I want that to change, though."

"Then it will."

"Just like that?"

"You're doing something about it. You could have refused to come today, or to meet the people you have so far."

She nodded reluctantly. "I suppose so. But my

behavior is so different from what it once was. I was accustomed to dealing with large numbers of people on a daily basis.''

Noah thought of her executive career. ''And you thrived on it.''

''Yes. But I can't resume my old life with my new face.''

He studied her expression. ''And if we succeed with the surgery?''

She looked pensive. ''I'm afraid to speculate on that.''

Spotting Cindy approaching, he didn't comment. If he succeeded with Grace's surgery, she would go back to Houston. He wasn't sure why that was unsettling.

After greeting Noah, Cindy linked her elbow with Grace's and together they strolled toward the deck.

Michael Carlson and Flynn Mallory approached Noah. Both were good friends. At one time Flynn had misconstrued Noah's friendship with Cindy.

But after Flynn and Cindy were engaged, Flynn thawed. And since their marriage, a genuine friendship had grown between Flynn and Noah.

Flynn glanced toward Grace, who was still chatting with Cindy. ''She's holding up pretty well.''

''It's early, though.'' Noah casually glanced in her direction, as well. ''I hope this isn't too much for her.''

Michael's gaze narrowed. "Is there more to you and Grace than doctor and patient?"

Despite his confused feelings, Noah shook his head. "No."

Michael's gaze reflected a shared understanding. "There's no crime in having your relationship evolve into one of another sort. I'm living proof of that."

Noah glanced at her again. "Even if she weren't my patient, Grace is a big-city woman. There's nothing for her in Rosewood."

"I wouldn't say that," Flynn interjected.

"Michael, Katherine's signaling for you."

"Ah. She probably needs help with the lawn chairs in the car."

As Michael left, Noah spotted his parents arriving. Of all the people he knew, his mother could best relate to Grace. But he also wondered if her residual scarring would be off-putting to Grace.

He kissed his mother's taut cheek. Her scars had never bothered him, other than for any distress it might cause her. However, Abigail Brady had assured him she was satisfied with her face. She had been an exceptionally attractive woman before the accident, but she hadn't mourned the loss.

Yet he had offered to find her another surgeon if she wished to pursue more restorative surgery. But she insisted she had made peace with the results.

His father, Joseph, glanced around the yard. "Hello, son."

"She's over there," Noah told him, reading the question on his father's face. "With Cindy."

"Your brothers and sisters should be arriving soon," his mother added. "Danielle has to work late, but everyone else should be more or less on time."

His pack of siblings were as different as the colors in a crayon box. But that made them more interesting, in his opinion.

"Dad, do you want to take a look at the barbecue pit?"

Joseph's glance was pointed. "Subtle, Noah. No problem. I'll make myself scarce while you introduce your mother to your young lady."

Noah raised his eyebrows.

"Fine," his father amended. "Your patient."

Joseph headed toward the old brick pit, and Noah's mother took his arm. "Don't mind your father. You know what a hopeless romantic he is."

"That's because he lassoed the greatest girl on the planet."

She smiled softly. "Don't tell him, but I got the best part of the bargain. So, how's Grace handling the barbecue so far?"

"She looked nervous when she arrived, but Cindy's put her at ease."

"It helps to have a friend."

"I'm hoping you will be one, as well," Noah confided.

"Let's see which way the wind blows, shall we?"

"Mother, I don't think Grace is so shallow that she'll pull back because you have a few scars."

"I'm not suggesting she is. But I remember how it felt at that stage—the fear, the disbelief. It's terrifying to believe you'll never be pretty again."

"You're lovely, Mother."

"And you're a sweet boy. But it's more than a *few* scars. Luckily, treatment has come a long way. And she's fortunate that you're her doctor." Abigail smiled again. "Now, hadn't you better introduce me to Grace before the rest of the pack gets here?"

"That's a wonderful way to speak of your other children," he said with a grin.

She raised one eyebrow. "*Other?* You're one of that pack."

Chuckling, Noah led her across the lawn. He was glad to see that Cindy was off gathering soft drinks. This was an introduction he preferred to have without an audience.

Grace turned toward him, glancing at his mother, as well.

Noah introduced them. To his relief, Grace smiled warmly at his mother. "I'm so glad to meet you, Mrs. Brady."

"Please call me Abigail."

Grace looked at the woman who had raised such a kind, strong son. And she saw the same qualities shining in her eyes. "I'd like that, Abigail."

Noah quietly moved away.

And Abigail studied Grace. "Noah was right."

Grace suddenly felt nervous. "About what?"

"You're warm and friendly."

Grace's lips trembled. "I'm afraid I haven't been since I've come to Rosewood."

Abigail nodded in understanding. "It's hard to be yourself when you're not sure exactly who that is anymore."

It was a tremendous relief to speak with someone who could relate so completely. "I haven't really been able to talk to anyone about it."

"Because they're eager to give you assurances they can't be sure of themselves. And they can't truly understand how it feels."

Grace sighed. "I know it sounds ridiculous, but it's as though I'm the first person who ever faced this. Of course I know I'm not—"

"But it still seems that way. And few of us have someone to soften the way, to clue us in on how we'll feel."

"I've had so many questions, so many doubts...."

Abigail met her eyes. "And those will continue

until you're certain of the final results. But that's not a bad thing. I'm convinced it's human nature. I can tell you it gets better, though.''

''Were you able to go back to your former life?'' Grace asked, hoping she wasn't offending the other woman.

''Yes. And it made me realize how precious each day is. And the feeling didn't fade. I still wake up mornings grateful for my husband and family, for all my blessings.''

Grace nodded.

''I imagine it's far too early for you to feel that way. You have more surgeries ahead of you. But luckily you have a premier surgeon to perform them.''

Smiling, Grace acknowledged the words. ''I think he's far more talented than the doctors in Houston. Look.'' With great effort she stretched the fingers of her right hand slightly. ''They told me this would never happen, but Noah refused to believe it.''

''That's my boy.''

''And he's an exceptional one.''

Abigail smiled, her voice soft. ''Yes, he is. Most surgeons of his caliber would still be living in a big city, raking in a fortune. I don't know if he told you, but when I had my accident, it bankrupted the family. All of our money was gone nearly at once with the overwhelming medical bills. And then there was the cost of moving to Houston to get the care I needed. The people of Rosewood donated enough money to make sure we had everything we needed. Without them, well…we might not be having this discussion. Their generosity made a huge impact on Noah. He was driven to give back to them. And he also wanted to make sure no other family had to go through what we did—being uprooted, leaving our home simply to get proper medical care. So he established a foundation.''

Grace was intrigued. ''I heard him mention the foundation once, but he didn't say what it was for.''

''It's to provide money for medical care to any Rosewood citizen who needs but can't afford it. Noah holds fund-raisers to bring in money for new equipment.''

''Is the foundation working?''

Abigail smiled. ''To date, they haven't turned away a single person in need. And our hospital keeps up with the evolving technology.''

''That's amazing.'' Grace met Abigail's gaze. ''You're proud of him.''

''He makes that easy.'' Abigail's voice softened. ''And Noah's proud of you.''

Shocked, Grace looked at her in surprise. ''Me? Whatever for?''

''Your courage. He knows from firsthand experience how difficult that can be to muster.''

"I don't have courage," Grace confessed. "I'm scared most of the time."

"It takes courage to simply be standing here today."

"That was Noah's doing!"

"You are a sweet girl." Abigail glanced over toward her son. "Noah was right about that, as well."

Grace guessed that the unbandaged portion of her face was pinkening with both pleasure and embarrassment.

"I was afraid you might have been put off once you saw me," Abigail continued.

Grace looked at her in astonishment. "Why?"

Abigail reached up to touch her cheek that still bore the scars of the explosion. "For obvious reasons."

"This may sound crazy—" Grace hesitated, "—but I could see the kindness in your eyes, and my first impression was how lovely you are."

Abigail's wise, knowing eyes misted. "You are a rare treasure."

Grace bit her lips, willing away the tears of sudden emotion. "I'm going all wobbly."

"Even strong women like ourselves need to lean now and then."

"Thank you for talking to me. I don't know if it stirs painful memories—"

"Not really. The pain is all in the past for me."

Grace wondered if she would ever truly feel that way.

Abigail glanced across the yard. "I'm glad you're up to meeting new people, because my clan's a crowd in itself. My husband and children are headed this way."

Grace could hear the fondness in Abigail's voice and she saw the love shining in her eyes. In that moment Abigail's scarring seemed to disappear.

Noah's siblings were as welcoming as he had promised. Their mother's accident had heightened their sensitivity. And to her relief, they acted refreshingly normal. They joked, laughed and teased her and each other.

It had been difficult to be treated as a fragile flower. Today she was an ordinary petunia, rather than a rare, exotic orchid.

Glancing around the yard, Grace marveled at the number of people she had allowed in her life because of Noah. It hadn't been that long since she had been frightened to meet Cindy. And the circle continued to widen.

These were good, kind people. They were far different from the people she had met while fast-tracking her career in Houston. Those people had sent flowers at the time of the accident, but not one had taken a personal interest.

Yet the people of Rosewood rallied like old

friends. Glancing across the lawn, Grace realized the force behind their commitment.

It was Noah who tied them all together.

An unexpected lump lodged in her throat. She was his project. Everything today was evidence of that—the carefully chosen guests, the talk with his mother.

For all that she was grateful to Noah for what he had done, she hated to think she had become a cliché. A patient becoming too attached to her doctor.

And a woman who could no longer trust her own judgment.

Chapter Nine

"I'm honored," Cindy announced the following week, studying her menu. "I've never been part of a therapy celebration."

"I hope I'm not being too optimistic," Grace replied. "But I have a good feeling about the progress with my hand."

Cindy nodded. "I can understand that. You have a great doctor."

Grace thought of all the stories she had heard about Noah from his mother and his friends. "He's beginning to sound like Saint Noah."

Shrugging, Cindy reached for a packet of sugar. "It's hard to find many men like him. He gives up his own social life to hold fund-raisers for his foundation. He's managed to involve the entire community in bake sales, car washes and festivals. Katherine says he does more on his own than her entire fund-raising committee for the church.'' Cindy stirred the sugar into her iced tea. ''And that's only one part of him. He volunteered to be the music director, and not only has it revitalized the choir, he's drawn in the youth. The church isn't large enough to afford a separate youth minister, but Noah's filled the gap. He has a natural way with young people. They trust him and he never lets them down.''

Grace thought of Patrick and how he had let her down. ''Noah sounds too good to be true.''

Cindy's expression grew contemplative. ''I suppose so. But he's for real.''

Grace drew a line through the drops of condensation on her glass. ''Do you see everyone this clearly?''

''Everyone, or men?''

Grace considered hedging, but Cindy was becoming a good and trusted friend. ''Men.''

''Ah. There I have less than twenty-twenty vision. You've heard my story. But I do have my moments. Why?''

Grace told her about Patrick, the plans they had made and her disappointment in him after the accident.

''Whew. That's tough. Do you think he just got

taken for a loop? That he really can come through for you?''

Grace hesitated. ''I keep wondering how I didn't see him clearly. And if that means I don't have the ability to judge a man for what he really is.''

Cindy searched Grace's eyes. ''Do you believe Patrick is without any merit?''

''I think he came upon the most difficult thing he'd ever faced and it was too much for him.''

''Could he have changed? Perhaps learned from it and grown?''

''Even if he has, I'm not sure I could ever get over my disappointment in him. And it's not because I don't believe in second chances. It's that I'm afraid I didn't know him as I thought I did.'' She rumpled her napkin. ''I agreed to marry Patrick— that should have been the most important decision in my life. And I made a mess of it.''

''I waited to marry because it was just as important to me. I thought I'd made an equal mess of things, too.'' She paused, then met Grace's eyes. ''But I never doubted Flynn.''

Swallowing, Grace nodded. She should have had the same faith in Patrick. ''How did you know for sure?''

Cindy's voice was gentle. ''I prayed about it. He's the only one who knows what our future holds, what is truly best for us.''

Grace didn't freeze. But her doubts couldn't allow her to agree, either. Surely a kind and loving God wouldn't want to steal away her parents one at a time, leave her alone, then subject her to horrific injuries that ended the career she loved.

"Why don't you try coming to church with me?" Cindy suggested. "You're not likely to work out your doubts about Him alone."

"It's not that simple."

"It rarely is." Cindy met her eyes. "Flynn no longer believed when he became part of my life. And it wasn't easy. He didn't wake up one morning and decide he was ready to accept the Lord again. He had to work through what had pulled him away. And they weren't little problems. It took a lot of forgiveness and soul-searching on his part."

"And now?"

"He's happier than he has been in decades."

Grace wished she could devise a happily-ever-after for herself. "I don't think that's going to work for me."

Cindy didn't press. "You'll know in your own time what will work. That's the beauty of it. All of the Lord's creatures are individuals with free will."

"Right now I have more questions than answers."

"I think that's true for most of us. And it's an

ongoing process. Because every day brings new problems, new questions.''

Grace thought of the crushing weight she had felt when her father died, when she knew she could no longer count on the faith of her childhood. ''I appreciate your advice, but it's not that easy for me.''

''I respect your decision, but if you want to talk to anyone who's been through the same experience, Flynn has a good ear. So does Michael Carlson.''

Grace frowned. ''They both had lapses of faith?''

''Big time.''

''But Michael's married to a minister.''

''Which is testament to the fact that even the most difficult situations have a solution.''

Grace wished that could be true for her, but she didn't believe it would. Still, she didn't want her new friend to feel rebuffed. ''I appreciate you lending an ear. And I'm glad it worked out so well for you and Flynn.''

Cindy reached for another packet of sugar. ''Perhaps it will work out for you as well...when you've decided who the right man is for you.''

Grace swallowed a sip of her soda, staring down at her bare left hand. She hadn't worn her engagement ring since the accident.

So who was the right man for her? One who had panicked?

Or one who had guided her over the most torturous route she had ever taken? The same one who was her doctor, she reminded herself. Who would no doubt be amused to learn that she had fallen into such an obvious trap.

But he couldn't find out—she owed him too much for his friendship.

And she was determined to keep it that way.

A few weeks later, Noah stood at the door of Grace's apartment, lifting his hand to knock. Before he could, the door whipped open.

Tim, one of the boys he knew from church, stood in front of him. "Hey, Noah!"

"Hi, Tim. I didn't expect to see you."

"Grace is tutoring me."

Noah blinked. "She is?"

"Yeah. Robert asked her if she would. I've got to get my scores up on my PSAT."

Still surprised, Noah nodded. "Sure."

Grace walked up behind Tim, her gaze going to Noah. "Hi."

"I didn't mean to come at a bad time. I had some extra time and thought we could get in a physical therapy session." Uncomfortably Noah realized he had come to feel proprietary about Grace's time.

"It's a perfect time. Tim and I just finished his lesson."

"See ya," Tim told them both, trotting down the stairs.

Noah still felt a bit confounded. "I didn't realize your tutoring program had grown."

She smiled. "I didn't expect it, either. But some of Robert's friends needed help, as well. And I've enjoyed it more than I thought I would. Come in."

He did, glancing around the tidy apartment, seeing the books and papers on the small table. "And you're all right about meeting new kids?"

"It's funny, but they don't seem to see the bandages. Even the larger ones after my last surgery. I thought it might be worse with teenagers, but their agenda is improving grades. Maybe it's because they're young that they are so accepting. And I work with each on a one-to-one basis. That makes it easier for me."

"That's great." He reached out, touching a leaf on one of the many plants. "You'll have a jungle in here soon."

"Everyone was so generous sending plants after the last surgery. It was especially sweet of your parents—since I'd barely met them."

"Mom said she feels like she knows you."

Grace's eyes softened. "We share a unique bond. And she was so easy to talk with."

"My friends always liked that about her," Noah agreed. "So, should we start on your therapy?"

"I already began."

Noah tried to disregard the prickle of disappointment. "Oh?"

"I made some lemonade. Juicing the lemons gave my left hand quite a workout. But my right one didn't cooperate. So would you like a glass?"

"Sure. I'm glad you're attempting more tasks."

Grace laughed. "I was, too, until I got to about the fifth lemon. Trying to hang on to the lemons with this stubborn right hand, twisting with the left, which is backward to me anyway... Well, I was about ready to start chucking lemons out the windows."

He found himself grinning. "I'd have loved to see that, especially if Ruth caught you midtoss. Trust me, she's merciless."

Grace continued laughing. "Yet you finagled her into growing blackberries."

"Not everyone has my touch."

"So you say," Grace retorted, handing him a glass of iced lemonade.

He held it up to the light. "Should I sift it for seeds?"

She wiggled the wooden stirring spoon at him. "At the peril of your own neck."

He tasted the lemonade. "Hey, this is good."

"Don't sound so surprised," she reproved him.

"And don't get too cocky or I'll draft you to head up a lemonade booth at the next festival."

Her expression turned thoughtful. "That would be fun, but I wouldn't be able to make enough lemonade with these hands."

Instantly he regretted taking her from her light, playful mood. "No problem. We always have volunteers who want to help out—not to mention an electric juicer. We usually have several people in each booth. You could supervise the setup and preparation."

She looked dubious. "And I could stay in the background?"

"If that's what you want."

"Hmm."

"We need to raise enough money to fund some pretty expensive testing equipment for the hospital. Refreshments have a high profit margin."

"If you really think I can help…"

"Don't try to back out," he countered, seeing the light of hope in her changeling eyes, wanting to keep it there.

Grace smiled in a shy fashion she hadn't employed before. "Okay."

"Give me a list of ingredients and I'll make sure they're at the booth."

To his surprise, she shook her head. "No. I want to do that, my contribution."

Although others often did the same thing, they were permanent members of the community with a vested interest in the outcome. "That's generous of you."

"No. It's generous of you to include me in the community. It makes me feel involved, useful." She glanced up at him. "I never learned how to be idle. I don't think I have it in me to be happy without working."

Instantly he thought of her career and all the big-city perks it offered. Things she couldn't be happy without.

Grace glanced at the clock. "It's later than I thought. Would you like to stay for dinner after therapy?"

"My parents are expecting me."

Her expression dimmed. "Oh."

"Why don't you come with me?" he found himself asking, hating to see the light go out of her eyes. "It's just a casual dinner."

"Your mother's not expecting me," she protested.

"With six kids, you always cook enough for anyone they might bring home. Mom still makes enough to feed a small army. And I know she'd be glad to see you."

Grace's eyes today were the greenish-blue of the

outfit she wore. They glided into the color of clear, warm ocean water. "It sounds like fun."

"It's noisy, somewhat crazy—yeah, it's fun."

Grace's lips rose in a smile. "Fun can be good."

Seeing the unaccustomed happiness dancing in her eyes, he agreed. "Yes, it can."

Grace wasn't sure exactly what to expect when she walked into the Brady home. But Noah was right. The noise hit her first. At least a dozen different conversations were going on simultaneously. And they didn't stop when she and Noah entered.

His mother noticed them, and a smile lit her face when she recognized Grace. Skirting the long table, Abigail approached them. "Grace, I hope Noah's brought you for dinner."

"If it's not any extra trouble."

Abigail laughed. "Never in this house. Even though two of my children have married, and they've all left home, I can't seem to cook in small portions." She took Grace's good hand. "You remember everyone, don't you?"

"I think so." Grace noticed that there was constant movement in the Brady home. Snatches of conversation floated by as the siblings caught up on the week's activities.

When she'd been young, Grace had dreamed of having a large family, a mass of brothers and sisters to enliven the house. But there had been no siblings. That was another prayer that had gone unanswered.

When they settled around the table, Abigail took the place at her husband's right. Throughout the chatter, laughter and clinking of china and silverware, Grace was aware of the tender looks that passed between the elder Bradys.

Grace couldn't help wondering just how Joseph saw his wife. Was he aware of her remaining scarring? Or did he still see her as his unmarred, beautiful young bride?

Either way, she guessed they shared an enviable bond. The house echoed with laughter, and their love had spilled over on their children. It was exactly the kind of home Grace had always dreamed of.

Noah leaned closer. "Do you feel like you're having dinner in Grand Central Station?"

"Yes." She smiled. "In a good way. It must have been wonderful growing up in a big family."

"I didn't know anything else, but I wouldn't trade any one of the aggravating, noisy lot. But I can remember envying friends with smaller families. At the time it seemed as though that meant they got a lot more than I did."

"And now you know differently," she guessed.

"The struggles, problems and joys you share have no equal."

Which was what Grace had imagined. "You have a lovely family."

Noah met her gaze. "Thanks. They mean a lot to me."

So much so that he had dedicated his life's work because of them. Grace admired his noble purpose, the fact that he hadn't let anything stand in his way. He possessed great strength, she realized yet again. A strength that drew her.

Once dinner was over, the family filtered off in many directions. With four pairs of hands in the kitchen, Grace could see her slow, awkward efforts weren't needed.

"Noah, why don't you show Grace around the property?" Abigail suggested. "Then we can have ice cream on the porch."

Noah glanced at Grace. "Sound all right to you?"

"Yes to both."

They left by the back door. Grace felt her feet sink into the lush lawn. A Victorian lamppost shed a circle of light near the house. In the distance Grace could see an aged gazebo. And as they strolled into the yard, she first heard, then saw a fountain of natural rock, the slowly moving water lapping over several levels of smooth stone.

Noah pointed out a neatly tended vegetable garden. "Ever since Mom's accident we've kept the garden going. We never had the severe money troubles again, but Mom and Dad didn't want to take any chances. And, in a way, it was our own victory garden.''

The scent of ripening cantaloupes and tomatoes reminded Grace of a charming farmer's market she used to frequent in Houston. She hadn't imagined the lure of having fresh fruits and vegetables just steps from the back door.

''I guess I've lived in apartments or condos so long I'd forgotten how special a garden could be. My dad and I planted a tree in memory of my mother in our backyard. He said that I could always reach out and touch the leaves, just as my mother was touching heaven.''

''That's a wonderful sentiment.''

It was difficult to dredge up a smile. ''I suppose so. But after he died I had to sell the house so that I could finish college. I wasn't able to touch the tree anymore.'' Nor her mother, or her father.

''There are times when I wonder why some people have so much loss and why others seem to go through life unscathed. But His plan's greater than we can see.'' Noah stopped. ''Sorry. I didn't mean to sermonize.''

She brushed away the clinging pain of the issue. ''It's all right. Just don't expect me to appreciate that plan.''

They strolled past latticework nearly obscured by

far-flung bougainvillea. "Everyone to their own time," he replied quietly. "Faith rarely works on a schedule."

If at all.

Moonlight streamed over the gleaming gazebo, making it look like a fantasy arbor.

Noah turned to her. "This was my parents' hide-out from us when I was a kid. I'd stumble across them every now and then. They'd be holding hands, talking. I used to wonder how they still had so much to talk about when they'd known each other forever." He chuckled. "Considering I was about twelve, fourteen years was definitely forever."

"It sounds as though they were very much in love." She thought a moment, then amended the words. "*Are* still in love."

"You see it?" he asked, surprised.

"Your father looks at your mother as though…"

"She never had the accident?"

Grace nodded.

"I don't think he sees the scars. I do know that he loves her just as much despite them. When she was hurt his biggest fear was that she would die. He never talked about the disfiguring. I don't think that was important to him, just that she survived."

Grace wondered how it would be to know such all-consuming love. One that didn't require explanation, but was a living, nurturing thing. Her mind flashed to Patrick's behavior after her accident, the difference a sharp pain. "That's how love should be," she murmured. "Just like your parents."

Noah met her eyes, his own dark with secrets she couldn't divine. "That's what I think."

Instantly Grace wondered if that was why he had waited so long to find just the right person, why he still hadn't found her. His parents' ideal was a difficult one to live up to.

"If your mother hadn't had her accident, do you think you'd have stayed in Rosewood?"

"That's a complicated question. I might have been lured to the big city, but I wouldn't have had the insider's knowledge I gained by moving there when I was in high school. Then again, I might not have had the opportunities, either."

"And if you hadn't had the opportunity?"

"I think you know what I believe."

The Lord's plan. "What if a person simply chooses to be daring and bold, picking his own career?"

"I imagine that's done thousands of times every day." He stopped beneath a towering magnolia tree. "Do you know how slowly these trees grow?"

Grace looked at him cautiously, aware of the sudden diversion. "Very slowly."

"This tree has been here for a great many years, growing stouter, taller. It seems so permanent that its destiny must have been preordained. But, in fact, a person planted the tiniest seedling.''

''Have you taken to speaking in allegories?''

''No, I've taken to walking in the moonlight.''

Grace swallowed suddenly, studying his face. She had been intensely aware of the stars, the moonlight. Of him.

Realizing the danger of her thoughts, she only smiled. Grace knew she couldn't let Noah know that her emotions were shifting, that her thoughts constantly turned to him.

''Are you all right?'' he asked quietly when she didn't speak.

She nodded, conflicted about her attraction to him.

As she glanced away from him, she saw a big dog running toward them, his tongue lolling to one side.

''Whoa,'' Noah commanded. But the large dog stopped by hurling himself at Noah, who took the dog's unwieldy weight with aplomb. ''Where you been, boy?''

The dog looked adoringly at Noah.

''Has he been out here all along?'' Grace asked, realizing she hadn't seen the dog earlier in the evening.

''Probably started chasing rabbits, then it got

dark. Columbus has a tendency to roam, always looking for new adventures.''

"Columbus?'' she asked, her lips twitching. "As in Christopher Columbus?''

"Yep. Spot didn't suit him, so…''

"He doesn't have any spots,'' she couldn't resist pointing out.

"Columbus is part Lab, part Boxer and part something only his mother knows. But apparently not a breed with spots.''

Grace knelt down, petting the friendly dog. Columbus in turn rolled over, presenting his chest to be petted. Grace obliged.

"You've made a friend for life,'' Noah told her, crouching down as well, watching as she and the dog became acquainted.

"Columbus seems to be a fine friend.''

Noah met her gaze. "So he is.''

Silence strummed between them, broken only by the sound of the dog's happy panting.

Grace felt her mouth go dry. Surely she imagined the flicker of interest in his expression, the darkening intensity of his eyes. She supposed all of his women patients fell for him. He was not only strong and handsome, he was their rescuer, the one who hoped to heal the worst of their wounds. Thinking it could possibly be more would simply open her up to more pain. And if he turned out like Patrick... It was unthinkable.

Rapidly she rose, afraid to elongate the moment.

Noah rose as well, the dog scrambling up beside them. "The ice cream's probably about ready."

Grace nodded, afraid to trust her voice, afraid it would reveal husky overtones of emotion.

Noah guided her toward the front of the house. "Everyone will be on the porch."

And they were, filling the glider, chairs and steps. Laughter and conversation colored the air.

"What kind of ice cream tonight?" Noah asked his mother.

"Peach. Took your brothers forever to get it all cranked."

"Cranked?" Grace asked in surprise.

Abigail smiled. "In some ways we haven't kept up with the passing centuries."

"She just spoils me," Joseph said, his arm around her shoulders. "No ice cream can compare to hers."

Grace thought of the kitchen in her Houston condo, equipped with high-tech appliances and yards of stainless steel. It had suited her in the city, but now its memory was stark in comparison to this home.

Noah scooped generous portions into two dishes. "I guess this all seems pretty small-town and hokey, doesn't it?"

She accepted the dish he offered. "What makes you say that?"

"I doubt you spent time eating ice cream on the front porch when you were in Houston."

"You're right. But—"

"You'll probably be glad to get back to the big-city pace after you've recovered."

Grace was saddened by the thought of leaving the close-knit community that had become home. "It's what I'm used to."

He nodded, then glanced at her bowl. "How's the ice cream?"

She dipped her spoon into the creamy mixture and tasted. "Incredible. It puts gourmet ice cream to shame."

"The peaches grow here on the property."

"This house seems to have everything," she murmured.

Again the moonlight seemed to fall between them.

"I always thought so," he replied quietly.

A few minutes later Abigail offered refills, which most everyone eagerly accepted. Grace could understand why her own appetite had withered, but she was surprised to see Noah refuse a second bowl.

When the gathering began breaking up, he glanced at her. "Ready? You have surgery on Friday. Probably shouldn't be up too late."

She nodded and they both rose.

Abigail turned to Grace, giving her a gentle hug. ''Now that you know the way to our home, you must come often.''

Pulling back, Grace warmed with heartfelt appreciation. As she turned, she met Noah's gaze and faltered. Somehow she didn't think he would be bringing her back soon.

And the pain of Patrick's rejection told her that was for the best. If only her heart would listen to her head.

Chapter Ten

Friday rolled around too soon for Noah. Flashes of the night he and Grace had walked in the garden had continued to nudge him. Pulling on a large reserve of self-control, he had cleared his mind to perform her surgery. But the fact that he'd had to do so kept his mood grim. Better than anyone else, he knew how crucial it was to keep his emotions and his job separate.

Glancing up, he saw the recovery nurse approaching on a run. "Dr. Brady. Recovery room two—stat."

Noah felt a chill in his blood that he remembered experiencing only once before. After he'd performed surgery on his girlfriend Jordan.

He pitched the chart he held onto the unit desk,

mindless of the rattling bang it made as it landed. Grace Stanton was in the second recovery room.

Noah's long strides outpaced the nurse's steps. The crash cart was in place beside the bed. Scanning Grace's vitals, he saw that they were plummeting. Memories assaulted him. In that instant Noah realized he cared more for Grace than he had Jordan. Terrified that he had made a fatal error, he read Grace's vitals again and found they were even worse.

As he quickly processed the possible causes, Grace flatlined.

Without hesitation he picked up the paddles. "Clear!"

The emergency team stepped back.

Grace's body jerked under the electrical charge. Noah held his breath.

One heartbeat registered. Then another.

Automatically Noah issued instructions for stabilizing Grace, forcing away any other thoughts. The team continued working on her.

As they did, Noah ordered more tests, determined not to lose her. Equally determined to find out what had gone wrong.

Training kept Noah's face noncommittal, his mind focused on Grace's survival. She looked so vulnerable, so alone on the gurney. She had been so very close to death.

He didn't leave Grace's side until hours later. Pulling off his sweat-soaked surgical cap, Noah exhaled. Now he could let his torturous thoughts run free.

He'd almost lost her. Another woman he cared about. And one frozen image kept coming to mind again and again—Grace's frightened eyes the first time he'd seen her, how the terror had turned to trust.

Trust he didn't deserve.

Knowing Ruth was waiting anxiously, Noah pushed open the heavy surgical doors. Mindless of the arthritis that plagued her joints, Ruth sprang to her feet. ''Noah?''

''She's stable,'' he replied.

''Something went wrong, didn't it? You said she'd be out hours ago.''

''She was.'' He pulled at the core of his strength. ''But there were complications.''

Panic flooded the older woman's face and her voice quivered. ''Grace?''

''She's all right. Now.''

''Oh, Noah. What happened?''

''An embolus, a blood clot, went to her heart.''

Ruth's hand flew upward to cover her mouth. ''No!''

''I won't lie to you. It was touch and go.''

''But I thought this was routine, without risk.''

He sighed. "No surgery is without risk. But you're right. This shouldn't have happened. I shouldn't have let it happen."

Ruth placed her hand on his arm. "Noah. I know this isn't your fault."

He stared ahead into the corridor. Now in the evening it was quiet, uncrowded. "Don't be so sure of that."

Ruth shook her head. "Noah, I trust you. That's not in question. I just don't understand how surgery on her face could cause a blood clot to her heart."

Noah felt the tension deep in the back of his neck. "I've ordered extensive tests. We'll know more after I get the results."

Ruth bit her lip, deep in thought. "Is it possible that the clot was caused by some of her internal injuries?"

"It's possible. I'm consulting with her surgeon in Houston." But he wasn't looking for an easy out.

"Noah, I've known you since you were a boy. I also know you did your very best in that operating room. Don't go looking for blame where there isn't any."

"We almost lost her, Ruth."

She squeezed his arm. "But we didn't. Let's concentrate on that."

Noah talked with her for a while, knowing Ruth

would stay around the clock until she was certain Grace was all right.

As he made his way to his office, Noah replayed the surgery in his mind, looking for errors, not able to find a satisfactory conclusion.

Only one fact could not be refuted. He had allowed himself to become personally involved with a patient. It had almost cost Grace her life.

Guilt and regret dominated every thought.

Hours passed, but Noah couldn't make himself leave the hospital. Instead, he kept in constant touch with the intensive care unit.

When that wasn't enough, he prowled the corridors, finding his way to Grace's side again and again.

Close to midnight, Noah walked soundlessly into the ICU. Grace's vitals had improved dramatically, yet he couldn't find peace in that yet. She was still in a remarkably fragile state. It would take so little to disturb the positive balance.

Long lashes shadowed her cheekbone on the unbandaged side of her face. She didn't have to open her eyes for him to know what they looked like. Her changeling eyes were like magic, blue one day, stormy gray another. They matched both her moods and her surroundings. He considered her eyes to be much like the opening of presents on Christmas morning. You might guess their color, or be completely surprised. Either way, it was like having Christmas every day.

Now, however, she was surrounded completely by white. Since she was in ICU, the lights were only marginally dimmer than during the day. There was no quiet, comforting hush of darkness to help her rest. Under constant observation, she couldn't be shrouded in anything other than light.

She slept deeply, a drugged sleep that kept her deathly still.

Grace had been through more than anyone deserved. And now this...

The soft scuff of rubber-soled shoes told him someone was approaching. Unwilling to allow his emotions for Grace to show on his face, he composed his expression and turned away from the bed.

"Dr. Brady. You have a phone call."

Thanking the nurse, Noah walked to the phone on the wall and picked up the receiver. "Dr. Brady."

"Hello. This is Patrick Holden. Sorry to phone so late, but I just got out of a meeting. I'm calling to check on Grace Stanton."

Noah wondered who the man was. "Information can only be released to a relative."

"Oh, well, I'm not...yet."

"Yet?"

"I'm her fiancé. I wasn't able to reach her aunt,

but perhaps you could ask Ruth to call me. She has the number.''

''Sure.'' Slowly Noah hung up the phone. *Fiancé?* How could he have spent so much time with Grace and not have known that important bit of news?

Walking back to Grace's bed, he studied her face again. What else hadn't she told him?

It wasn't only her career that was calling her back to Houston, but a man she had pledged her heart to. It should be a relief, he told himself. He couldn't be distracted by a woman who was engaged. His professional and personal lives wouldn't face the threat of being commingled again.

Feet suddenly leaden, he forced himself to relay the message. He told the nurse and then watched her step outside to locate Ruth.

However, it wasn't relief he felt. He couldn't turn off the feelings he already had for Grace.

A woman he apparently could never have.

Still, he returned to her side. At least while she was sleeping she couldn't see the truth in his face.

Grace sighed, a small sound that pulled at him.

He continued to watch her as he wondered about Patrick Holden. And why Grace had never mentioned the man.

Two days later Grace awoke in that peculiar state that felt as though she were both leaden and floating.

It was the medication, she knew. That had been explained to her before.

The previous day had been a blur. Vaguely she remembered they had moved her from one place to another. The room she was in had the familiar look of all the other hospital rooms in the past months.

Unable to remember what Noah had said, she wondered how this surgery had gone. She lifted her left hand, now completely free of bandages, to hesitantly touch the new bandages on her face. She couldn't tell anything from the tentative examination. The bandages did seem thicker. But that happened after each surgery.

Glancing to one side, she saw Ruth slumped in a chair, having fallen asleep while she stood guard. Grace felt a wave of appreciation for her aunt, who had assumed this burden without a moment's hesitation or complaint.

Although her head felt heavy, Grace turned it, seeing several vases of flowers. She couldn't imagine who had sent them all. She also wondered why she felt so weak.

A muted tap sounded on the door, so quiet she could barely hear it. Her own voice was almost as quiet. "Come in."

Looking uncertain, Robert poked his head in. "Is it okay?"

Grace cleared her throat, yet her voice wasn't much stronger. "Yes."

"They said at the desk that you could have visitors, but I didn't want to wake you up."

"You didn't," she assured him.

He pulled a bunch of handpicked flowers from behind his back. "These are from my yard."

"They're beautiful," Grace replied, touched by the boy's gesture.

He glanced over at the vases of florist-arranged flowers. "Mine can't compare to those."

"And none of those were handpicked just for me." She sniffed the bouquet, lush with fat roses. "Nor do any of them smell so wonderful."

Robert grinned. "How do you feel?"

"Kind of woozy right now. But it's taking me less time to recover each time."

"Have there been many surgeries?" he questioned, his eyes filled with curiosity.

"I'm afraid so. It's not something Noah...Dr. Brady can repair quickly."

"He's the best," Robert replied. "A lot of adults just see past teenagers, you know? Like we're some sort of herd instead of different people."

She nodded.

"He doesn't." Robert hesitated. "And you don't, either."

Grace felt a rush of emotion. "Thank you, Robert. That means a lot to me."

He looked embarrassed, but pleased. "When are they going to spring you?"

She smiled at his choice of words. "I'm not sure. When I know, I'll phone you about resuming lessons."

"Okay." He looked over at Ruth, who was still sleeping. "I mowed the lawn this morning early. I hope it's okay."

"I'm sure it is. You know my aunt Ruth. She'll tell you if it isn't."

He grinned. "Yeah. Well, I'd better get going."

"Thanks for visiting, Robert. And for the beautiful flowers."

"Sure." He disappeared quickly, the limit of his teenage self-consciousness reached.

Ruth spoke from the chair, surprising Grace. "So, I'd let him know, huh?"

Although exhausted, Grace smiled. "I wondered how you slept through that exchange."

Ruth stood. "Figured the boy didn't need an audience. Bringing flowers to a teacher is traumatic enough without a witness."

"He's a sweet boy," Grace replied.

"Well, don't ever tell him that! You'd ruin his teenage standing." Ruth moved closer to the bedside and picked up Robert's flowers. "How are you feeling this morning?"

"A little tired," Grace admitted. "Silly, I know. I barely woke up."

"I'll ring the nurse."

Grace glanced around, wondering why they were surrounded by so many machines. "I don't need anything," she protested. Seeing the lines on her aunt's face, Grace reached for Ruth's hand. "You didn't have to stay so long. You're the one who must be exhausted."

"Nah. I'm a tough old bird. Besides, I'd only worry at home."

Grace felt another rush of gratitude. "I'm glad you're here."

Ruth smiled at her niece. "Good. Because you're not getting rid of me."

The nurse entered, going to the bank of machines surrounding the bed, making adjustments.

"Will I live?" Grace asked, wondering again why she had so many more machines this time.

The nurse didn't smile as Grace expected. "You're on a steady course, Miss Stanton." She looked over at Ruth. "I'll let Dr. Brady know she's awake."

Grace wondered why she was suddenly out of her own medical loop. "Ruth?"

Her aunt turned, walking toward the windowsill

where several flower arrangements had been placed. "Do you want to know who these are from?"

Distracted, Grace nodded. "There's quite a collection."

As expected, there was a large arrangement from her employer. There was also a tall, dramatic arrangement of exotic flowers from Cindy and Flynn Mallory, and a flourishing, glossy-leafed plant from Katherine and Michael Carlson. Noah's parents had sent a spring bouquet filled with bright color.

Surprised and touched, Grace listened as Ruth read all the cards. She came to the last one, roses from Patrick.

Ruth hesitated after reading the card.

"What is it?" Grace asked, seeing something else in her aunt's expression.

"Patrick called to check on you."

"Oh."

"I haven't called him back yet. I thought you might want to do that."

"Could you handle it, please?"

Again Ruth hesitated. "Fine. But he'll call again."

"I can't face hearing his excuses just now. I only want the truth from now on." Grace closed her eyes. "Just the truth."

Chapter Eleven

Noah stared at the book in his hands, not seeing the words. His focus was shattered. It had begun to fissure immediately after Grace's brush with death. When he was away from the hospital, it was all he could think about. What if Grace hadn't made it?

He had replayed Jordan's death a hundred times since Grace's surgery. All the what ifs, the unanswered questions.

Noah knew he had to put those thoughts aside so that he could find the best doctor for Grace. It would mean she would return to Houston, but that was a small price for her to pay to receive top-notch care. Glancing at the pages of names, Noah knew he would recommend only a precious few. He had already spoken to his first choice and Trevor Scott had agreed, despite a long waiting list, to add Grace to his caseload.

Now he just had to tell Grace.

Knowing he couldn't put off giving the news, he replaced the book on the tall wooden shelves flanking the door and left his office.

It didn't take long to reach Grace's room. Shaking off any personal thoughts, Noah adopted his most professional mode as he pushed open the door.

Looking somewhat stronger, Grace smiled when she saw him.

Ruth's tired expression lifted, as well.

Noah kept his tone benign. "How's the patient today?"

"Okay," Grace replied. "How's the doctor?"

"Fine." He moved to the bank of machines, noting the readouts.

"Don't feel you have to elaborate on that," Grace told him, her voice puzzled.

"I'm here to discuss your health, not mine." He was glad to see that the purplish tinge beneath her eyes had faded.

Ruth drew her brows together, but remained silent.

"Your vitals look good," Noah reported, wondering if Grace was strong enough yet to learn about her close call.

"Good." Grace glanced over at her aunt. "Now

maybe Aunt Ruth will stop fussing. She's been acting as though this were my first surgery, instead of the zillionth.''

Noah met Ruth's gaze. ''There's a reason for that.'' He paused. ''Grace, everything didn't go well this time.''

Her fingers flew up to touch the bandages.

''The restorative work wasn't the problem.''

Grace's eyes widened, but didn't show fear. ''Then what?''

''A blood clot. It was nearly fatal.''

Puzzlement rather than the expected shock entered her eyes. ''But I'm all right now?''

''At the moment.''

''Noah—'' Ruth began.

''Grace deserves the truth, as well as the best care possible.''

''That's what I'm getting,'' Grace protested.

''No. Rosewood Hospital is an adequate facility. But we can't compete with the Houston Medical Center. There you will have the best of the best, both in completing your restorative work as well as making certain you don't have any more residual effects from your internal injuries.''

''Noah Brady!'' Ruth chided.

''You said nothing went wrong with the surgery on my face.'' Grace struggled to sit up straighter. ''And this hospital's been just fine so far.''

Noah's face and voice remained tight. "Hardly. I've been consulting with your surgeon in Houston, apprising Dr. Burger of the developments in your case."

He was shocked to see a wave of hurt flash in her eyes. "I'm not going back to Houston."

"I don't want to be blunt, but you don't have a choice in the matter. I'm turning your case over to Dr. Burger."

Ruth took a step toward him. But Grace's words hit him first. "You can send every X ray, test and file you have on me to Houston. But I'm not going."

He tamped down his frustration. "There's no point in being stubborn."

"You walk in here and announce that you're shipping me back to Houston, that I have no say in the matter, and you call *me* stubborn?"

Noah knew this was an argument he had to win. For her sake even more than his own. Not only had he crossed the line by having feelings for her, those feelings had grown beyond caring. Beyond anything he'd expected. "Grace, the issue isn't debatable."

Determination replaced the hurt in her eyes. "I'm not a package you can pop in the mail."

Noah turned to Ruth. "Will you talk to her?"

Ruth's expression filled with disappointment. Disappointment in him, Noah realized.

Realizing he could say no more that would convince her, Noah left Grace's room. His heart heavy, he kept seeing the hurt in Grace's eyes. Trust had turned into pain. And he had only himself to blame.

A week later, Grace was relieved to be back home. In Ruth's home, that was. Her aunt hadn't been willing to let her stay alone in her apartment the first few days. Ruth had been hovering ever since Noah had dropped his bomb.

Grace couldn't understand why his defection hurt so. She now knew that men couldn't be trusted. Despite that, she had begun to believe that perhaps Noah was an exception.

And she had no idea what she was going to do about her medical care. Noah maintained that he wasn't going to change his mind. Grace couldn't imagine leaving the safety Rosewood and her aunt offered. The thought of facing strangers in the city horrified her.

The doorbell rang, and Grace couldn't stop the spurt of hope that it might be Noah. She heard a masculine voice mingling with Ruth's. But it wasn't Noah.

"Hello, darling," Patrick greeted her.

"Patrick."

He didn't seem to notice the lack of enthusiasm in her greeting. "Looks like you came through it all right."

She wondered briefly if he knew she'd nearly died. As quickly, she decided it really didn't matter. "Yes. I'm fine."

He angled his head, studying the bandages. "Looks like you have more wrappings on your face than before."

Grace kept her tone even. "That happens after each surgery."

"So, you're just skating through the surgeries?"

Ruth made a strangulated sound.

Patrick turned to stare at the older woman. "What?"

Ruth sent an apologetic look to her niece. "Grace had complications."

"What kind?"

"Just a clot," Grace answered mildly.

He glanced again at Ruth. "That so?"

Grace let Ruth off the hook. "Apparently it could have been serious."

Patrick frowned. "What does your hick-town doctor say about this?"

Grace squashed down the sudden impulse to defend Noah.

But Ruth didn't have the same self-control. "Noah Brady is an excellent surgeon! In fact, he wants to send Grace to the medical center in Houston to make sure it doesn't happen again."

"Finally!" Patrick replied. "I guess you're relieved, aren't you, Grace?"

She clenched her teeth. "Not exactly."

"Patrick—" Ruth started to add.

"No offense, Ruth, but this is hardly the place for Grace to get the medical care she needs. This Dr. Brady—he's the only plastic surgeon in town, right? No one to consult with? I know you like the guy, but that doesn't mean he's qualified. Besides, Grace doesn't belong here. Her life's in the city."

Grace stared at Patrick, unable to believe how entirely clueless he was. Again she wondered how she'd come to be affianced to a man who knew so little about her. "Patrick, I don't intend to return to the city now."

"You're being ridiculous," he replied.

Stung, she stared at him.

"Sorry. Didn't mean to be so blunt. But you've got to face facts, Grace. If this doctor thinks you need more competent care, then you'll have to go to the city."

Her back up, Grace made a sudden decision. She wasn't leaving. Neither Noah or Patrick could force her. If Noah refused to treat her, she would find another way. But she wasn't going to be pushed into a corner. "I'm afraid not, Patrick."

He let out an exasperated hiss. "I don't understand you anymore, Grace."

She kept a bitter laugh contained. "Anymore?"

Shaking his head, he stared at her. "You're not thinking clearly. Maybe after you've had time to really process what this means you'll come to your senses."

Grace felt the same overwhelming disappointment she had since the accident. Knowing that, she remained silent.

Patrick stood suddenly. "I rescheduled a meeting to come here today, but it appears to have been a waste of time."

Even though she knew he wasn't the man she'd thought him to be, his words hurt.

He pushed a hand through his immaculately styled hair. "Didn't mean it that way, Grace. Look, I'll get going and we'll talk when you're feeling better."

He strode to the door, Ruth trailing behind him. This time Grace didn't even glance toward the window to see him leave.

Ruth returned, her expression somber. "I admire your pluck, Gracie. But what are you going to do if Noah won't reconsider?"

"That can't be an option," Grace replied with far more assurance than she felt.

The church sanctuary was quiet, still. It was a time Noah savored. Although he valued the fellowship of fellow members, he could always reach deeper to what was in his heart when alone.

Choir practice would start in just over an hour. Until then he could relish the solitude. He sat in a pew, rather than at the piano. But the peace he expected didn't descend on him. His troubled emotions were still irretrievably tangled.

Deep in thought, he was surprised when a shadow fell over him. Glancing up, he was even more shocked to see Grace.

"What are you doing here?"

"Hello to you, too," she replied mildly, glancing at the empty space on the pew beside him. "Can I join you?"

He nodded. "I wasn't expecting anyone."

"I know."

Thoroughly baffled, he studied her expression. "You do?"

"Cindy told me. She said that when your schedule permits, you like to come here before choir practice."

"Ah. Not too many secrets in a small town."

"But plenty of good friends."

He eyed her warily. "Yes."

"I thought you were my friend."

Her arrow hit his already wounded heart. "Yes."

"And my doctor."

He could feel the scowl as it crossed his face. "Not anymore."

"So you're willing to concede that the doctors in Houston were right? That I'll never regain full use of my hand?"

"Of course not."

Her eyes shifted color. They were pewter now, and challenging. "Then how am I supposed to regain its use without you?"

He hesitated. "I'll help with your hand, but that's all."

"So you're going to make house calls in Houston?"

Angered frustration edged his voice. "You're treating this as though it's some joke. We almost lost you, Grace. Don't you understand that?"

She gasped, a soft mewing sound. Wary tenderness lingered in her expression. "You say that as though you care."

"Of course I care."

"Then help me. I don't want to go to another doctor, someone who looks at me as just another patient—"

"That's exactly what you need!" He didn't care that he'd raised his voice enough to shatter the hushed quiet of the sanctuary.

"You'll have to explain that."

"Grace, no doctor should allow the line between

personal and professional to become blurred. I knew that, but I still did. Four years ago I was crazy about a woman in Houston—Jordan Hall. I thought she was everything I'd ever wanted—talented, compassionate. She was beautiful, too. But she didn't think her beauty was perfect. Essentially she blackmailed me into performing frivolous cosmetic surgery.'' Remembering emphasized the raw pain his mistake had caused. "And she died."

Grace's hand reached out to cover his. "I'm so sorry, Noah."

"Me, too. I vowed then it would never happen again."

"But you were in love with Jordan," Grace protested.

He stared into her eyes, now soft silver, glowing with compassion. "So I was."

Grace glanced away and he felt the blow to his heart.

"Noah, you told me there's just one final surgery. I don't want another doctor."

He shook his head. "That's impossible."

"Look around you, Noah. Can you sit in this church, the one you've urged me to return to, and refuse? Is that what the Lord would want you to do?"

Shaken, he examined her expression and found

only sincerity. "Don't ask me to risk your life again, Grace."

"And if He asks?"

Noah had no answer. Only the realization that whatever he decided, it could mean the life of the woman he loved.

Chapter Twelve

Only a few weeks later, Grace could scarcely believe it. Her tutoring had grown, one student at a time, from two to eleven in a relatively short time. And she was continually receiving inquiries to tutor even more children.

Caught up in the demands of her former career, Grace had almost forgotten her love of literature. Before her father had died, she had planned to become an English teacher. But her focus had changed. Teaching had become intertwined with the pain of her past. So Grace had left that decision behind with the rest of her dreams.

Now she wondered. How different would her life have been if she had allowed herself to pursue the course she had initially planned? Even though she

was only their tutor, Grace found immense fulfill-
ment in teaching her pupils. Could that sustain itself
on a full-time basis?

Hearing a knock on the door, Grace glanced at
the clock. She wondered who it could be. Perhaps
Robert, hoping to put in another hour's work. But
she didn't mind. He had proven to be not only bright
and quick—he also challenged her. And he nudged
her memory, reminding her how it had been to be
his age.

She whipped open the door. But her smile faded.

"Hello, Grace." Patrick stood at the top of the
stairway, favoring her with his boyish grin.

Instinctively she took a step back. "Patrick. I
wasn't expecting you."

"I took a chance that you might be home."

Reluctantly she gestured to the living room.
"Come inside."

He followed her, looking around at her tiny apartment. Mentally she followed his thought process,
seeing him size up her new accommodations that
were a far cry from her sleek Houston condo.

"Not what you expected, is it?"

He shrugged. "I doubt there's much to choose
from in a burg this size."

"Perhaps you shouldn't judge something you
know nothing about."

"I didn't come here to fight, Grace. I know things

haven't been right since the accident, but it's taken me a while to process all the changes.''

''And you've worked them out now?'' she asked, feeling at once angry and vulnerable.

''Not completely. But I'm trying, which is more than I can say for you.''

''Excuse me?''

''You don't seem very happy to see me when I come to visit.''

''This hasn't been a particularly *happy* time for me, Patrick.''

He gestured around the apartment. ''You act as though you like this place, this town. It's not you, Grace. None of it. Your career, your friends, everything you could want is back in the city.''

Grace pictured what he described, what she'd given up.

''I can tell you're thinking about it. I don't know what hold this town has over you, Grace, but you can shake it, move on.''

She reached up to touch the bandaged portion of her face. ''Not quite yet.''

''I'm going to be visiting on a regular basis until we can straighten this out.''

Patrick and Rosewood. The two didn't seem to belong in the same sentence, Grace thought inanely.

''Why don't we take a walk?'' he suggested.

"Maybe you can show me what it is you like so much about this place."

Reluctantly she agreed and they drove to Main Street. It seemed awkward. Both because she was with Patrick and because of the noticeable bandages on her face.

He was looking at her now as though trying to read her mind. "Penny for your thoughts."

"They're not much of a bargain."

He didn't try again. Instead he parked in one of the many open spots. They strolled beneath the full, tall trees that lined Main Street. Dusk was descending, but it didn't discourage the shoppers and strollers.

Early fall in Rosewood dictated baseball and ice cream. Since the game was finished for the day, most of the spectators gravitated toward the ice cream parlor. Built in the 1800s, the quaint old place boasted a marble fountain, tall bar stools and root beer floats big enough to dive into.

"This place is hard to believe," Patrick commented. "Looks like a movie set from about sixty years ago."

Grace tried not to take offense at his words. "The pace is slower here."

"Slower? I think it's stopped completely."

She felt defensively protective about the town that

had opened itself so warmly to her. "That's not really fair."

"It's picturesque, I suppose. But surely you're about to go stir-crazy." Another expression overtook his face. "Unless it suits your recuperation."

Grace hid the grimace she felt. Why was it that Patrick's every reference to her injuries grated?

When she didn't reply, he looked pained. "I don't know what to say to you anymore. Things seem so different."

"Things *are* different. *I'm* different."

"But you'll be back to your old self soon."

Grace felt the truth pushing at her. "No. I won't. Not just on the outside, either."

"What do you mean?"

"I've changed."

His expression grew thoughtful. "That makes sense. It would be difficult to go through that much pain and not be affected. But you're still *you*, Grace."

She couldn't really argue with that logic. "I suppose I am."

"You've been thrust into a different set of circumstances that seem appealing because you've been recuperating."

Grace started to shake her head.

"Think about it," Patrick argued. "Don't you miss your job, the adrenaline rush of pulling together events the entire city talked about for weeks?''

"You're not suggesting that I can just step back into my old job?"

"You told me they're holding your position open."

She met his gaze. "And you expect me to stand in front of huge groups of people with my scars all aglow?"

He couldn't disguise his horrified reaction, though he tried. "Maybe you could have an assistant do that part of your job."

"An assistant that good would be capable of doing the job on her own."

"Well, something related, then."

"Patrick, everything about PR means people contact. You know that."

"Don't just dismiss it out of hand."

"Out of hand?" She looked at him with disbelief. "I've lived with what's happened to me on a daily basis. While you were 'working things out' I was having surgeries and treatments. It didn't go away for one minute of one day. So don't think you can assess the situation in a matter of minutes."

"I wish I could turn back the clock, make things better for you."

Struck by one of his few empathetic responses,

she felt her anger deflate. "Thanks. But there's no point in trying to wipe away the past months."

"You act like you don't want to forget. Is there something else you're not telling me?"

Immediately she thought of Noah. "It's not just one thing. I'm not the same person I was when we planned to get married."

As they walked together, Patrick didn't attempt to take her hand. He acted as he had since the accident—as though if he touched her she might break. Bewilderment and irritation had segued into sadness. Was this how all men saw her?

Even as the thought progressed, she had an instant image of Noah as he took her hand and made her feel like a real person.

Grace heard someone call her name.

Cindy and Flynn Mallory, along with their children, had spotted her. Glancing over at Patrick, she saw his surprise.

"Does everyone in town know everyone else?"

She resented the irritation in his voice. "It's a very social place." Still, Grace was relieved that Patrick behaved in a charming manner when she introduced the Mallorys.

"We're headed toward the ice cream parlor," Cindy was saying.

"I'm having sprinkles," one of the triplets announced. "Bunches of 'em."

"That sounds wonderful," Grace replied, capti-
vated by the children.

"Would you like to join us?" Flynn asked.

"Yes," Cindy encouraged. "Please do."

Grace knew Patrick would play along, but she
also knew he wouldn't mix well with the Mallorys.
"I think we'll enjoy walking for a while."

Cindy picked up on Grace's mood, smiling gra-
ciously. "Enjoy. It's a beautiful evening."

Patrick watched the Mallorys as they walked into
the ice cream parlor. "Rosewood's a real family-
oriented place, isn't it?"

"Now that you mention it, I guess it is."

"You didn't notice it before?" Patrick asked in
surprise.

"Not particularly." She paused. "Does that
bother you—the family thing?"

"No. Just that in the city we socialized with other
career couples who understood our goals."

Goals she hadn't examined closely in a while.
Goals, it occurred to her, that she'd never questioned
before.

They continued walking, glancing at the store-
fronts and the other people who strolled down the
quiet street.

"I wonder what it would be like growing up
here," Patrick speculated.

"Comforting," she replied, realizing the word

had slipped out without thought. Then she remembered Noah's words. "And fulfilling."

Patrick's eyebrows drew together. "Fulfilling? I doubt there are a lot of opportunities here."

"I suppose that depends on your definition of opportunity." Grace thought of all the people who came together to help each other as well as members of other communities. Her tutoring had been an incredibly satisfying experience.

Patrick looked at her as though she were a stranger. "I thought we agreed on what we believe opportunity is. A chance to grow in our careers, to establish contacts, to build our lives."

Had that once been so important to her? To build her life solely through her career? "I don't see things like I once did," she admitted.

"I've read that people who are ill… I mean have a long recovery, well, that they're not always themselves for a while."

Her smile was sad. "Who do you think I am, then?"

Patrick looked as though he wished he knew.

Grace took pity on him. "Perhaps you're right."

He brightened a fraction. "It's a big adjustment. I know that."

For which one of them? Grace wondered. And why did the prospect fail to stir her?

As they strolled farther down the street the conversation dwindled to nearly nothing.

And though she walked beside Patrick, he didn't occupy her thoughts. Instead her mind filled with a sudden desire to see Noah. Logically she couldn't reconcile the two, but her heart wasn't listening.

Chapter Thirteen

Noah was pleased by the attendance at the festival fund-raiser. It wasn't a surprise. The townspeople always supported the events that funded their hospital.

As he walked toward the refreshment booths, Noah told himself it was to check on all of them. But he headed straight for the lemonade stand Grace was supervising.

He had called and given her an out in case she didn't want to participate. But Grace had insisted. She hadn't wanted to be involved in taking the drink orders or ringing up sales—that was still too public.

Although Ruth was with her, Noah was concerned about how Grace was handling the festival. It was by far the largest public event she had attended. Per-

son by person she had eased into the community.
But this was a giant step.

Noah found her at the back of the booth, mixing
a batch of lemonade. Ruth was at the opposite end
of the same table. She'd had the foresight to bring
a juicer to speed up the process.

"Hello, ladies."

Grace glanced up, the unbandaged side of her face
flushed. "The lemonade's selling well."

"I'm not surprised. It tastes great."

She smiled, her bottom lip trembling a fraction.
"How about a complimentary glass?"

Searching her eyes, Noah felt a fist of emotion hit
his gut. This was real. She was that singular woman
he had searched for all his life. He cleared his throat.
"Sure."

Grace poured lemonade into a paper cup. "We're
using crushed ice. That's part of my secret."

He lifted the cup to his lips, realizing he could be
swallowing kerosene for all the attention he paid to
the drink.

"What do you think?"

"Wonderful," he murmured, swamped by his
feelings for her. Then he settled his voice into a
more normal tone. "Really wonderful."

Her smile spilled sunshine across his soul. "I'm
glad."

As Grace held his gaze he saw questions flicker

in her expression. She gestured vaguely toward the batch of lemonade. "I should be—"

"Sure. And I have things to check on."

Her eyes didn't leave his. "Of course."

Noah made his way out of the booth, conscious of Grace's gaze still fastened on him. It wasn't until he'd walked to the other side of the festival that he realized they hadn't discussed anything medical…or personal.

And that maybe, just maybe, he had a chance.

Inside the lemonade booth Ruth studied Grace's face. "Have you told Noah about Patrick?"

Grace slowly shook her head. "I never considered it an issue. You know, it's funny. Immediately after the accident all I dreamed of was having Patrick come after me, realizing he couldn't live without me. I wanted him to be my knight on a white horse, charging in to claim me, to proclaim his undying love regardless of what had happened."

"And now?"

"Now I realize that he never was the knight-on-a-white-horse type. I expected qualities he didn't possess."

Concern hovered in Ruth's eyes. "What about Noah?"

"I'm sure he can have his pick of whole women."

Gently Ruth tipped up Grace's chin. "Regardless of how your injuries heal, you *are* a whole woman. A woman any man would be proud to call his own."

Tears trembled in Grace's eyes. "I wish that were so." She bit her lips to stop their quivering. "Oh, how I wish that were so."

Chapter Fourteen

The church was quiet. Midweek, early in the day, few people came to the sanctuary. Noah knew that he could have chosen somewhere else to conduct Grace's therapy. But he continued to hope that her contact with the church would bring her closer to reconciling her faith.

"Have you thought any more about attending church?" he asked.

"Have you reconsidered your decision to remain as my surgeon?" she countered.

For the next few moments the only sounds between them were the random notes of the organ as Grace picked through an unfamiliar song.

She reached for a higher note on the organ than

usual. "I can stretch my fingers farther than the last time without any pain. I've been able to for days."

Surprised, he stared at her. "Why didn't you share that with me?"

She kept her head averted. "It's not always easy to tell something, even when you want to."

Noah felt a familiar fist to his stomach. "Such as?"

Finally, reluctantly, she lifted her head. "I haven't told you about Patrick…my fiancé. Well, he *was* my fiancé. I'm not sure exactly what to call him now."

"No, you haven't told me about him."

She swallowed visibly. "When I first had the accident, Patrick came to the hospital. But he was shaken, unsure of himself, of what had happened. He said that he wanted to stand by me, but the look on his face… He was horrified. I could see that he couldn't deal with my accident."

"And then?"

"It was as though he didn't know how to deal with me once I was disfigured—like I wasn't the same person."

Noah silently called the man a fool, but aloud he forced himself to remain neutral. "And now?"

Grace went very still. "He keeps coming to Rosewood."

Noah felt the crush of conflicting emotions. "To pick up your relationship?"

"So he says. I'm sorry I didn't tell you earlier about him."

"It wasn't essential to your recovery."

She cast her face downward, seeming to stare at the keys of the organ. "No. I don't suppose it was."

"I imagine you and he share a lot of common interests, living in the same city."

"I suppose so," she murmured. "Patrick wouldn't fit into a small town."

Noah hid his flinch. No doubt Patrick would find them all backward and hokey. "Not everyone does."

Grace lifted her face, her eyes searching his. "No. I guess not."

He wanted to tell her that she fit, though. That everything about her was right for Rosewood and for him. But in light of her revelation about Patrick, he knew it wasn't the honorable thing to do.

Instead he gently touched her hand, positioning her fingers over the organ keys. On the outside he remained professional. But inside he could feel the quaking of his heart, the splinter of its breaking.

The quiet sanctuary seemed to welcome the mellow notes of the organ as Grace picked them out with more and more certainty.

And Noah tried not to dwell on how forlorn the lonesome sounds would be without her.

Chapter Fifteen

Grace hadn't ventured to Noah's house on her own before. Aside from the barbecue, she had been there only to sit in on a few band practices.

But she felt compelled to come here, to speak with Noah. She needed answers to the questions Patrick continued posing. Grace hesitated as she approached the house. The side gate to his backyard was ajar. On instinct, she stepped through.

She could see Noah beneath the tall chinaberry tree at the edge of the lawn. Smoke curled lazily from the massive brick barbecue pit. But the table wasn't set up for entertaining.

Still Grace was hesitant as she approached, not wanting to intrude on anything he had planned.

Before she could speak, he turned, as though

sensing her presence. He looked surprised, but not displeased.

"I took a chance you might be home," she began, feeling suddenly nervous. "Your office said you were off today. Am I interrupting anything?"

He shook his head. "I was about to put a burger on the grill for lunch. Should I make it two?"

"Okay. Can I help do anything?"

"Eat," he replied.

She relaxed a fraction. "Do you always fire up the barbecue pit for just yourself?"

"Depends. Sometimes I think the great smell beckons company."

"Cross my heart, I headed over here *before* I smelled the mesquite."

His gaze met hers. "Either way, you're welcome."

Her throat dried and she found it difficult to swallow. All the words she had rehearsed fled. "You have a way about you, Noah Brady."

His eyes darkened. "A good way?"

A very good way. But she could only nod.

Their gazes connected. Noah finally broke the moment. "Would you like some iced tea?"

She welcomed anything that would relieve her emotion-parched throat. "Please."

It didn't take Noah long to fetch the tea. Standing beside him, she sipped the sweetened brew. As she did, Grace listened to the bright chirping of the birds, the quiet sounds of the occasional car that drove down the street.

Noah stirred the fire. "It should be ready soon." Then he turned toward her. "I have the feeling that you've got something on your mind."

She fiddled with her glass for a moment. "Noah, can you tell me why you're so content in Rosewood?"

He didn't answer immediately. And his voice was slow when he did reply. "Well, you know about my mother and family, my debt to the community."

She leaned forward. "That's *why* you're here. I suspect you've repaid that debt a dozen times over. Yet you stay. What is the source of your happiness?"

He met her gaze steadily. "The true source of all my happiness is the Lord. He makes everything else possible. Friends, my work with the youth in our church, the caring attitude of the community."

She was silent, considering his response.

"Grace, I know you don't like to talk about it, but can you tell me why you've drifted away from your faith?"

She wanted to close up as she always did, but this was the man who had shared the worst of her fears. Her voice stumbled as she began. "I was eight years old when my mother died from cancer. I questioned why God let her die. My father told me that it was His will, that we didn't always understand it, but we had to accept what happened. When I didn't want to accept it, my father promised that I would never be alone. He said that I could get through my mother's death and any other bad thing because he would always be there for me, to help me understand God's will." Grace paused, remembering the pain— old, but still sharp. "When I was eighteen my father was killed in a small plane crash."

Noah stepped closer. "I'm sorry, Grace."

Ridiculously, she felt the sting of tears over what had happened so long ago. "I know it sounds childish, but I clung to that promise, and when my father died it shattered my world. I couldn't understand why God had let that happen."

As her tears increased, Noah put his arm around her shoulders, bracing her up.

Grace released words she had kept locked up for years. "And even worse, it was as though God had betrayed my father, as well. I couldn't understand why He made my father break his promise."

"Oh, Grace." Noah pulled her close, letting her cry against his shoulder. He didn't offer platitudes or false comfort.

The hot rush of tears dampened his shirt, yet he held her. And she didn't sense any judgment from him. Finally she pulled back, needing to know. "Do you think less of me?"

"For suffering terrible losses and losing your way?"

She ducked her head, then slowly lifted her face to look at him. "The accident was the final straw. It seemed that neither God nor Patrick wanted to stand by me."

He flinched, and instantly she regretted her mention of Patrick.

Yet Noah ran his hand gently over her disheveled hair. "You're weighted by burdens greater than we can bear alone."

"I just don't know," she murmured, wanting to have the trust he did, but burned by her past.

His pager beeped and Noah sighed. "It's like a fifth appendage." He scanned the digital readout, his face tightening.

"What is it, Noah?"

"A train wreck. It's bad. Lots of injuries. I've got to get there right away. I'm the emergency medical coordinator."

"Let me come with you," she offered impulsively.

He frowned. "Bystanders get in the way."

"If I can't help, I'll leave," she promised. Grace flexed her bad hand, demonstrating its improved state. "And I can do *something*."

"All right. But you can't allow ash or any other foreign matter to get past your bandages—you'd be risking infection. Understand?"

She nodded, following as he jogged to his car. Once inside, she glanced back at the house. "Oh! What about the fire in the barbecue?"

Noah was already backing up. "The advantage of an old brick pit. It's completely contained. This isn't my first emergency when I had it going. The fire will burn itself out."

Speeding down the quiet residential street, Grace felt a sudden qualm of fear, envisioning a derailed train scattered over the surrounding homes. "Could anyone in town have been hurt by the wreck?"

"Not likely."

The possible effects of the tragedy kept them silent as Noah raced through the town. A few blocks from the site, a burning stench filled the air. Glancing over at Noah, Grace saw his face tighten even more.

The train was derailed. But the actuality was far worse than what Grace had imagined. It wasn't only the smoldering heaps of twisted metal. Shattered glass covered the ground. And personal belongings were strung out like a macabre yard sale.

Wounded and dazed passengers struggled to stand. Others wandered aimlessly, ineffectually trying to stanch flowing wounds.

Horrified, Grace followed Noah as he grabbed his medical bag and jumped from the car, running toward the fire chief. Immediately Noah drafted two paramedics. "We have to set up a triage," Noah told them. "On this side of the big oak." He glanced up at the fire chief. "Is help on the way?"

"I've contacted all the surrounding towns, but no one can get here for hours." He didn't have to say that distance was the problem.

Noah snapped open his cell phone, punching in numbers. "I'm going to call for help in Houston and send our helicopter."

Relief flashed over the chief's face. "Good thinking. This is bigger than anything we've ever handled."

"Call the school and city hall. Have them make announcements and ask for volunteers," Noah told him. "I'll phone the hospital, ask them to call in all off-duty staff."

As the chief nodded, Noah spoke into his cell phone, getting arrangements for the helicopter going.

Grace was filled with admiration for his competence and leadership. Looking around, she desperately wanted to help and not be in the way.

Noah closed his cell phone.

She spoke quickly. "Noah, would it help if I guided the walking wounded to a safe place?"

He rapidly scanned the area. "Over by the tree next to the big oak. It's close enough to where we're going to set up triage without getting in the way. Have them sit and keep still."

Then he was gone, searching for the most seriously wounded.

Grace walked quickly toward the train. Suddenly a flashback of her own accident hit with such intensity that she felt her knees buckle. Calling on her strength, Grace straightened, determined not to give in to the weakness.

Seeing a woman wandering toward her, Grace quickened her stride and gently took her arm. "Ma'am?"

Dazed, the woman remained unfocused.

"Let's get you to a safe spot." Grace spoke softly, sensing the woman's shock. Glancing up, she saw townspeople running toward the railroad tracks. Many carried first aid kits. Others brought pillows and blankets.

Michael and Katherine Carlson arrived. As Grace helped the woman, she saw the duo check with Noah, then begin organizing the volunteers.

An ambulance screeched to a stop, the attendants jumping out. They headed toward Noah. It seemed everyone knew that he was in charge.

Grace settled the woman and went to fetch another person.

As she did, Cindy rushed up to her. "Katherine sent me over here to help you. They're not sure how many people may be ambulatory."

"Are you here alone?" Grace asked, not seeing Flynn.

"Since we have a plane, Noah called Flynn and asked him to organize the other small planes at the airport to fly to nearby towns and collect help. Houston's sending help, but this is massive."

Grace looked out over the wreckage. "It's the worst thing I've ever seen. There seem to be far more patients than doctors and nurses."

Cindy nodded grimly. "Thank the Lord for Noah." Then she left to help an elderly man wandering nearby.

By the time Grace returned to help another possible patient, there were as many townspeople as passengers in the scattered wreckage.

A nurse had been assigned to oversee the passengers brought to the safe spot beneath the tree, separating out those who needed to be sent to triage.

Between Noah and the volunteers he put in charge, the damaged landscape soon began resembling a *M*A*S*H* unit. Still the cries of the wounded, along with those of frightened babies and children, mingled with the shouts of volunteers and firemen.

The most seriously injured began to be transported to the hospital via ambulance as well as by volunteers with vans and SUVs.

Why had this happened in Rosewood? she wondered. It was too small to handle something so massive, so horrific.

Just then Grace spotted her aunt. She was organizing a pillow-and-blanket brigade.

Suddenly an explosion rocked the ground, pitching Grace off her feet. Stunned, she lifted her head and saw that one of the engines had blown. New shards of glass and metal spewed out, a free fall of blowing shrapnel.

Immediately she looked for Ruth, her heart in her throat. She couldn't bear to lose this one last member of her family. Surely God wouldn't be that cruel. Not seeing Ruth, Grace felt a sob crowd her chest. Weakness started to overtake her. Then she spotted Ruth being helped up by a young man.

Scrambling to her feet, Grace looked up to see Cindy's concerned face.

"Are you all right?" Cindy asked, holding out a steadying hand.

"Yes. You?"

"It scared me to death." Cindy squeezed her hand in encouragement.

Grace left her and ran across the sandy width of the railroad embankment. Reaching Ruth, she hugged her, silently uttering thanks for her aunt's safety.

Pulling back finally, Ruth tried to scold, but her voice betrayed her concern. "Child, what are you doing in the middle of this mess?"

"Same thing you are."

Ruth's eyes ran over Grace, making sure she was okay. "I guess you come by it naturally. Be safe, though."

Grace hugged her again. "You, too." Then she ran toward someone who was stumbling from the nearest train car.

She helped that man and the next. Person after person until she wondered how there could be so many of them.

Hours must have passed, she realized later. Because ambulances and paramedics from the closest towns had arrived.

And a second plan was already taking shape. Members of the community volunteered to open their homes to the uninjured. Grateful passengers left with their new sponsors.

As the sun began setting, Grace met up again with Ruth.

Looking fatigued, Ruth patted Grace's arm. "Grace, I want to do something, but I'm worried about you."

"Me?"

"Yes, dear." Ruth hesitated. "I'd like to offer our home to some of the passengers."

"Of course," Grace agreed instantly. "But why are you concerned about me?"

"Well...the accident, the reminders."

"Bad things are always going to happen." Grace swallowed. "I know that. But I can't hide from life forever. It's funny, you know. Since we arrived at the train wreck, I haven't thought once about my bandages, about what people would think."

Ruth took her hand. "I wish you knew how very special you are, child."

Grace smiled. "If so, I came by it naturally."

Ruth smiled at the echo of her own words. "Then shall we bring home our guests?"

"I suppose you have someone already picked out for us to take home."

"You'll like them," Ruth assured her.

Grace spared one more glance in Noah's direction, knowing he must be tired, also knowing he wouldn't stop until the job was done. In that instant Grace realized she'd never known a man like him. A man of noble purpose living a life dictated by honor and faith. A man determined to keep her at arm's length.

Chapter Sixteen

It took a while for Rosewood to settle back to normality. The uninjured train passengers had returned home and only a few remained at the hospital. Which meant Noah had time to seek some solace.

Normally he could find that at his own home or at the family house. But discontent traveled with him. So he had come to the church for the peace he needed.

Once inside, he passed by the pews, going instead to the organ. As he played the last song he'd practiced with Grace, he pictured her hands stretching for the notes. She had persevered beyond the pain, determined to make the hand work normally again. He could envision her earnest expression, the determination in her eyes.

Caught up in his thoughts, Noah was startled to feel a gentle touch on his shoulder. Abrupt silence replaced the music as he whirled around.

"I'm sorry to disturb you, Noah." Grace looked at him with those entrancing eyes. "Please continue playing."

Unable to pull his gaze from her face, he gestured to the bench. "No, this is your song."

"Oh." Hesitantly she sat beside him, flexed her fingers and began to play.

Her hair smelled of vanilla, he decided. A scent so delicate he might have imagined it.

Grace finished the song, and the final notes trailed off in the surrounding silence.

"How did you know I was here this time?"

She smiled, a tremulous lifting of her lips. "You weren't at home, so I drove on. Your car's parked out front."

The distinctive Porsche. "Hard to miss."

"Yes." She fiddled with a slender bracelet on her wrist.

He hadn't seen that piece of jewelry before. Stiffening, he wondered if it was a gift from Patrick. "Is that new?"

Grace glanced down as though surprised to discover the unconscious gesture, and stilled her fingers. "No. Very old. My father gave it to me."

Instantly he remembered the pain she associated with his passing. "It must be very special."

She nodded, then lifted her head, seeking his gaze. "Noah, I need to talk to you."

His gut tightened. Was she about to tell him that she'd decided to marry Patrick? "What is it?"

"I've come to ask you to reconsider your decision to not perform the final surgery."

He wondered how relief could blend so completely with angst. "Grace—"

"Don't answer just yet. I know this is a difficult decision. But I need you."

"I can't understand why you won't go to the doctor I've recommended. He's the best—"

"He's not you," she replied with quiet conviction. "And I'm guessing you've followed my progress since the last surgery."

Since Grace refused to see the other doctor, Noah had had an associate monitor her case as she'd come in for regular bandage changes. "I've already made my decision."

"I've made one of my own, Noah. If you won't perform my final surgery, I won't have it done."

"That's ludicrous! You're so close. Why would you risk the final outcome?"

Grace met his gaze. "I've had a lot of trouble with trust since the accident. And I trust you. Not a strange doctor in Houston. *You.*"

He wondered at the undercurrent of her words. "I've explained before why this is impossible."

"Only if you make it so."

"You're not listening, Grace."

Her eyes pleaded with him. "You're wrong. I've listened to your reasons for not performing the surgery. I've also listened to what you've said about the Lord. And now I'm wondering…have you listened to Him, as well?"

Noah thought of the chaos his thoughts and feelings had been in. Maybe Grace was right. "I don't know."

"Noah, it has to be you."

He met her gaze, feeling lost in her eyes, finally speaking reluctantly. "I'll think about it."

"Oh, Noah—"

"I said *think* about it. And pray."

She placed a hand over his. "That's all I can ask."

No, she could ask for his heart and it would be hers.

Grace stood. "I'll leave you alone, then."

Noah watched as she left. It was a decision he couldn't put off. And one that Grace was right about. It was time to take it to a higher power.

Noah stared at Grace's still body. Still but healthy. There had been no surgical complications this time, no clots that threatened her life.

Choosing to perform her surgery had been one of the most difficult decisions of his life. But after prayer and reflection he knew it was the right one.

She stirred.

Noah stroked her arm. "It's all right, Grace. You're going to be fine this time. I'm watching out for you. No matter what you decide, no matter who you choose, I'll be there for you. Always."

It wouldn't be long until she awoke. And based on her current progress she would be transferred to a room shortly afterward.

Noah added another blanket, knowing she would be chilled. He also knew he should move on, attend to other things, but it was difficult to leave her.

The recovery room was cold. Grace shivered beneath layers of blankets. The room echoed with the sound of beeping machines and the faraway buzz of voices.

She'd had an accident, Grace realized. A terrible accident. In a train. Or a car.

But that was an opportunity.

Opportunity? The word floated in and out of her consciousness.

A deep male voice spoke her name and soothed her. It was a voice she knew. Her knight, she recognized. Noah, not Patrick. He would spirit her away and make everything all right.

Because it was his opportunity.

No, hers.

The machines beeped more loudly. Her aunt Ruth must be worried, she thought, the fog of anesthesia still clouding her mind.

But she shouldn't worry.

Because it was an opportunity. Noah had said so.

That evening Grace's hospital room was quiet, the door closed against the intrusive noise of the corridor. And in the solitary confines of her room Grace had been thinking. She remembered the word that had been on her lips from the moment she awoke.

Opportunity.

And she didn't think it was the vague wanderings of her medicated state. In the time since Noah had told her that his service was an opportunity, the concept had been nagging her.

And now she knew. The car accident wasn't God's punishment. It was His blessing. Tears slipped down her face, wetting her bandage, salting her lips.

If not for the accident, she would never have come to know the joy of living in a caring community of friends. Or the simple joy of a day, unrushed by a pace spiraling out of control. Nor would she have rediscovered her dream of teaching.

And she would never have met Noah.

Grace stared out into the darkness beyond the window. He had changed her life in ways she was just now beginning to understand.

Hearing the door open, she withheld a sigh. She knew they had to come in often. But sometimes she felt like a Sunday roast, being prodded, her temperature checked, everything short of being basted. Silly thought, she realized. Much like the first one she'd had about Noah.

"Grace?" Noah spoke softly.

"The blackberry doctor," she blurted out before she could stop herself.

In the low light she could see the gleam of his teeth as he grinned. "I'd been advised your anesthesia had worn off. I'll have to recheck your chart."

"I didn't think I'd see you tonight."

He glanced about the empty room. "I can't let my favorite patient fend for herself."

Her voice was soft. "Is that what I am? Your favorite patient?"

Noah studied her face. "You're a strong, courageous woman who I admire tremendously."

Without warning, her lips trembled.

He stepped closer, his face drawing into a frown. "What is this? Tears?"

"No…" She began to protest.

But he had already perched on the side of the bed, reaching out to gently wipe away her tears. His touch was a balm to more than her physical wounds.

And he didn't speak for a long while, allowing her to recover her calm.

When she had, he met her eyes. "Would you like me to sit with you for a while?"

Suddenly that seemed like the best thing she could imagine. "It's late," she protested weakly. "I imagine you're tired."

"No," he corrected her. "Not just late, *very* late."

The stars seemed to pop out, one at a time, while she listened to Noah as he told her warm, comforting tales. She wasn't sure if it was the medication or her newest revelations, but never had she felt so secure.

And for just this time she could believe it was forever. That, somehow, Noah might come to love her as she loved him.

Grace's postsurgery hospital stay was without incident. However, even once she was home, the time seemed to pass in an excruciatingly slow manner. She still avoided mirrors, yet she was conscious of her appearance nearly every moment.

Because this was it.

In a matter of days she would know her fate.

She couldn't help picturing Noah's expression when her bandages came off for the final time. Would his eyes fill with understanding and sad kindness? Then her stomach would lurch as she envisioned pity.

And her mind filled with her rediscovered faith. All along she had believed she was battling outside forces—the accident, fate—but she knew now that wasn't true.

She had been battling inner demons.

Ones that had been with her since she lost her faith. In some ways she wanted to share her discovery with Noah. However, it was still too new, too fragile.

Grace also knew she could pick from a dozen other people—Ruth, Cindy, Katherine and more—to discuss her faith. But she needed more time to reflect, to hold the revelation close before she shared her feelings.

Patrick called from Houston, and Grace realized she was already treating him like a friend. Without knowing it, she had distanced herself emotionally from him long ago. Since the last surgery she had searched deep in her heart. It truly wasn't a grudge and it was no longer a matter of his betrayal.

Grace wanted a deep and abiding love. One that would remain strong as they grew old together, one that could withstand anything, no matter how bad it was.

She wanted Noah.

The phone rang. When she heard his voice, her hands began to shake even though she knew he couldn't truly read her thoughts.

Noah was calling on his cell phone. He was in his car, only a few blocks away. Grace agreed to his stopping by shortly for her therapy. Replacing the receiver, she stared at her hand, the scars still red. Angry, her mother used to call scars. Red and angry.

It wasn't often she could remember her mother's words. She had died so very long ago. And it occurred to Grace that she never associated memories of her mother with anything other than pain. That really wasn't fair to the wonderful woman her mother had been.

Her smile had been wide and quick. She had laughed a lot, Grace realized. Warm, caring, her arms always ready for a hug. The pain had come only once she was gone. But that shouldn't have been her legacy.

Hearing a car in the driveway, Grace knew it was Noah's Porsche. The distinctive engine couldn't be mistaken.

Her heart quickened as it never had for any other man. And she rushed to the door, opening it just as he reached the top of her stairs.

"That's getting to be a habit," he greeted her.

Embarrassed, she stepped back. "My mind's so full, I think it's spilling over."

He didn't seem to find that particularly strange. "Filled with what?"

"I was just thinking about my mother, actually." She took one of the chairs and he followed.

"And?" he prompted.

"Just that in the past, whenever I've thought of her, all I felt was hurt and loss." She paused. "And today, just now, I was thinking about her smile. It was wonderful."

Noah's eyes met hers. "I can almost see it."

"And her laugh," Grace continued, caught in his gaze. "It was magical."

"Yes," he agreed.

She pulled her glance away, trying not to reveal her feelings. "And until today I never thought it odd that I only remembered the bad."

"And now you do?"

Grace remembered. "My mother was so special. Why do you suppose I didn't think about that instead?"

His gaze was thoughtful. "It's my feeling that faith helps us deal with the loss of loved ones. It's difficult to think about them if you don't believe you'll eventually be reunited…if you're not certain they're in a better place."

"I just always thought of her as gone," Grace said, realizing this suddenly. "Forever."

"You asked me once how I could believe," he said quietly. "I don't understand how someone can't. It must be a very difficult life."

She swallowed. "I'm beginning to think you might be right."

Hope flashed in his expression. "Grace?"

"I'm not sure I'm ready to talk about it."

He searched her face, his own filled with understanding. "That's okay. It's enough that it's in your thoughts."

Ridiculously, she felt tears threaten. How did he always know the right way to respond to her? And how would she ever replace him in her life?

But he didn't let her wallow in her emotions. "Have you kept up your stretching exercises this week?"

She managed a wobbly smile. "Yes. I didn't want to get in trouble with my doctor."

"Pretty tough, is he?"

"Murder," she replied, grateful for his light tone.

"Then we'd better start working." He took her hand, holding it a bit longer than necessary before starting the exercises.

She felt her pulse increase, and her throat was dry. Unable to speak, she followed the slow movements of his hand over hers. She wasn't sure whether she was relieved or disappointed when they moved to the piano.

Surprisingly, Noah began playing. It was a song she had never heard, but she liked the gentle, evocative tune.

When the last notes faded away she glanced up at him. "I like it, but I haven't heard it before."

"I'd be surprised if you had. It's one of mine."

"I didn't know you composed music!"

"Time restraints don't allow for it much anymore."

"Did you write this one a long time ago?"

His expression grew more thoughtful. "No. I was inspired to write it recently."

With a sickening thud she wondered if he had written it for a special woman in his life.

Noah didn't speak for several moments, either. And when he did, he surprised her. "Would you like to play something?"

Usually he made her go through scales and other stretching techniques, waiting until the end of the session for the free play. But she didn't protest. Instead she chose a piece that had been her father's favorite. It always comforted her.

When she finished, Noah was quiet again.

"Is something on your mind?" she asked softly.

"Just restless tonight." He turned toward her. "Would you like to play hooky?"

Grace took heart. "Doing what?"

"Taking a drive…maybe a walk by the lake."

He had combined two of her desires. To be away from anything to do with her injuries…and to be with him. "I'd like that."

They drove through the uncrowded streets. Children played on well-tended lawns and older people sat on their porches, watching the day end.

"Everything seems back to normal," she marveled, calmed as always by the peaceful town. "It's as though the train wreck never happened."

"Quiet, nothing happening."

"I meant that in a good way," she protested.

He glanced over at her. "You won't get an argument from me."

They approached the vintage downtown center, and Grace remembered Patrick's unwelcome comment. "Someone told me he thought Main Street looked as though it had been plucked from an old movie set."

"I guess it does." Noah turned in the direction of the lake. "Never thought about it before. It's just the way Rosewood is."

The road curved, the incline increasing, then dipping as they passed through the gently rolling hills. Huge fields of long grass carpeted the knolls and tall trees congregated over the last of the summer wildflowers.

Feeling as though she'd had her eyes opened for the first time in many years, Grace saw there was beauty all around her. As she watched, a deer darted from the scrub oak, then loped up the hill.

"Look!"

His gaze followed hers. "White-tailed deer. They're all over these hills."

"I had no idea."

Noah turned on to the road leading to the lake. "All kinds of wildlife out here."

"The closest I used to get to wildlife was the poodle in the condo next to mine," she admitted.

"I didn't know a poodle was considered a wild animal."

"You don't know Bootsie," she replied. "That dog went nuts over everything and nothing."

He smiled suddenly.

Seeing the grin, she smiled herself.

Then they were on the last turnoff that led to the lake. It took only a few minutes to reach the shore. Climbing out of the car, they started walking by mutual, silent accord.

They left the gravel road and climbed toward the sandy banks. Tall stalks of reedy grass fluttered in the mild breeze. A pair of mallards chattered at each other.

"They sound like they're arguing," Grace said as she watched them.

"It's the last of the season for them. They'll be flying farther south soon."

That took her aback. "The months have passed more quickly than I thought."

He remained quiet for a bit as they strolled farther along. Then he looked at her. "The next few days will pass just as quickly."

Swallowing, Grace tried to read the subtext of his words. And again she wondered how he would react to her final appearance. "Actually, the days are crawling."

"Not like in Houston with a busy pace and a rewarding career to fill the days."

Days that would never be repeated. But Noah wouldn't want to hear that. It sounded too pitiful. And pity was the one thing she didn't want from him.

The sun had begun its slow descent. The golden rays gave way to pink-and purple-tinged fingers in the sky.

Noah glanced over at her. "You're quiet."

She pushed away her thoughts. "Just rediscovering how beautiful everything is."

He looked surprised. "It's the same as it was the last time we were here."

But then she hadn't considered the gifts of life. "I didn't really see it before."

Noah searched her face, but didn't question her.

Instead they continued walking, accompanied only by the sounds of the last birds of the day singing their final songs.

And the silent echo of Grace's longing for the man who had gone from rescuer to mentor…to thief of her heart.

Chapter Seventeen

Patrick glanced around the room. "I didn't think the restaurant would be this crowded."

"I've been out in public since the accident," Grace reminded him. "It doesn't bother me as much now."

"Hmm." Patrick didn't meet her gaze, instead studying his menu.

It hit her a beat later. Patrick was embarrassed.

She closed her own menu. "We don't have to stay."

"Of course we do. You said we needed to talk. And I'm ready to listen." He met her gaze and had the grace to look ashamed. "Sorry, Grace. I'm just not accustomed to this yet. It will take some time."

She didn't reply.

"Think there's anything on the menu that won't clog our arteries?"

"I'm sure they'll have something," Grace murmured, wishing Patrick didn't have to pick the place to pieces.

"Don't you miss decent restaurants?"

"Not particularly. Rosewood has a lot to offer in so many other ways."

He groaned. "I'll have to take your word for that. I can run an extra two miles tomorrow to work off this dinner."

She wished her troubles could be solved so easily.

"Is something wrong?" Patrick asked when she remained silent.

"Not wrong exactly." She met his gaze. "My last surgery was probably the final one."

It was difficult to read the stream of emotions that crossed his face. But his voice was cautious. "Isn't that a good thing?"

"Yes. But this is pretty much it. I'll know the results, good or bad."

"I know I blew it before, Grace. But I won't this time."

She looked deeply into Patrick's eyes. He was doing his best to be sincere, she realized. It wasn't his fault that she no longer fit into his well-ordered life.

Although she'd once thought she loved Patrick

enough to accept his proposal, her original feelings for him paled against those she had for Noah.

She loved the person Noah was. A man who gave up riches to devote his incredible talent to his small town. One who volunteered for the church, helped children and teenagers, and whose heart was true.

A man who possessed the courage, strength and nobility that she now knew was paramount to her happiness.

"Grace?"

"This may be hard to believe, but I don't have any hard feelings about what happened before."

He pushed aside the dinner plate and leaned forward. "Good. This time—"

"Patrick. Please don't."

His face went still. "What do you mean?"

"I want you to believe that I truly don't hold a grudge. But I can't plan a future with you. I've changed."

"I told you I could deal with it," he protested.

She bit her bottom lip. "That's not the change I mean." Gathering her courage, she lifted her gaze. "I don't love you, Patrick."

He looked stunned. "This is just a reaction to your final surgery."

Grace shook her head. "No. Regardless of how the surgery comes out, I'm sure."

"This is because of the way I acted immediately after the accident, isn't it?"

She searched for the truth. "Partially, but I really have changed."

He still looked stunned. "I can't believe that I'm not going to be part of your life."

Grace glanced down, fiddling with her fork. "Please don't make this more difficult."

He stilled the nervous gesturing of her fingers. "Okay, how about a truce for the evening? I promise to be on my best behavior."

"Okay." She hadn't really wanted to accept his invitation, but he had been insistent. "I haven't asked. How have you managed to take so much time off from work? You've been popping up here to Rosewood on a regular basis."

"I shifted some of my accounts to Stevenson for the interim. He thinks they're his for the long run, but—"

"He thinks wrong," she finished for him, with a smile for remembered times. "He doesn't have your talent or your tenacity. They're still your accounts."

"Tenacity. My best quality, you once said."

Grace looked at him, sad for what they had once had. "You have many great qualities, Patrick. That's not why my feelings changed. It's about me, about how different I am now."

"Quite a truce, isn't it?" he said wryly.

"I do think it's one time your tenacity isn't going to work."

"You're so sure?"

"Absolutely. Patrick, I think it's time for you to go home."

"But your bandages come off in a few days."

She sighed. "I know. But either way, I'm not resuming the life I once had. And, generous as your offer has been, I don't need your shoulder. I've come to peace with my accident…and the near certainty that I'll be disfigured."

"But—"

Grace took his hand. "I've found something else here in Rosewood, Patrick. My faith. And that's going to enable me to deal with whatever happens."

"You shouldn't be on your own."

"Don't you see? Even if I didn't have Ruth and all the wonderful, caring friends I've made here, I've got the Lord to lean on."

"Grace—"

"Please. Do it for me, Patrick. I would feel better knowing you're home, doing what you love, doing what you're so great at."

"You're a very special woman, Grace." Belated regret simmered in his eyes.

She leaned over, kissing his cheek. "Goodbye, Patrick."

As Patrick clasped her hand for the last time, another man watching from the entrance turned abruptly and left the restaurant as quickly as he had entered.

Once outside, Noah sucked in deep breaths of the fresh night air. And called himself a fool.

The following days crawled for Grace.

On the day before her bandages were to come off, she had scheduled only two tutoring sessions in case she had any last-minute errands or qualms. Now Grace wished she had filled the day with lessons.

Ruth had questioned if she would be all right with a little company for dinner. Grace welcomed any distraction.

She had hoped that Noah would call. But the phone was remarkably still. Of course she would be seeing him the next day. Still, she had thought he might offer some words of encouragement.

Glancing at the clock, she realized enough time had passed that she could go over to Ruth's to help with dinner.

A wheelbarrow and garbage can blocked the path to the back door. Guessing that her aunt must have some project going, she headed for the front door instead.

She heard a flurry of voices and realized the guests had already arrived. An apology for her tardiness on her lips, Grace rounded the corner into the living room.

A circle of women stopped talking and broke into applause.

Stunned, Grace stared at them.

Ruth and Cindy walked out of the group, each taking one of her arms.

"What is this about?" Grace asked, still baffled.

"We're here to applaud your courage," Cindy explained.

"And tell you how much we love you," Ruth added, her eyes glistening with a sheen of tears.

Katherine approached. "You've been a wonderful example for all of us, demonstrating grace, courage and strength. And we want you to know that our hearts will be with you tomorrow."

Grace felt the tears slip from her eyes as she looked at these women who had become so dear to her. "I *never* cry," she finally managed.

Everyone laughed, surrounding her, offering hugs and hankies. These were the women Grace had joined to make memory books for a town that had been flooded, losing all their sentimental treasures. She had been part of their efforts to help the victims of the train wreck, gathering clothing, providing a warm, welcoming home. These and other projects had woven Grace into their community. And tonight she knew that wasn't a temporary thing, that she was truly part of the town.

"This is so amazing," she told Ruth after a few minutes. "Thank you."

"You've always touched my life, child. Now you've touched theirs, as well. I'm so proud of you."

Grace swallowed the threat of more tears. "I'm going to be completely waterlogged soon."

Ruth hugged her. "I'll settle for that."

A delicious-looking buffet had been laid out on the dining-room table. And each woman had written her a few special words on slips of paper. All the papers had been placed in a heart-shaped container of cloudy pink glass.

"When you need a pep talk, or a smile, or to know we're close, just pull out one of the slips of paper," Cindy explained. "And know you're in our hearts."

Incredibly touched, Grace accepted the gift, knowing she would treasure it as she did these friends.

Memories, dear to each person, spilled out as they talked and talked. And by the end of the evening Grace was overwhelmed by the outpouring of support.

"We'll be praying for you," Cindy and Katherine promised as they left.

And Grace knew she would be doing her own praying, as well. It would be a special prayer. One for herself, it was true. But not for an unscarred face. Rather for an unscarred love.

The morning dawned, bright and clear. Grace's appointment was early, just after Noah completed morning rounds. Ruth accompanied her to his office.

When Grace's name was called, Ruth clasped her hand. "Do you want me to go in with you?"

Grace shook her head. "No. I need to do this by myself."

Both understanding and concern hovered in Ruth's eyes. But she squeezed Grace's hand one more time before releasing it.

Noah didn't make Grace wait long in the examining room before he joined her.

"Hi," she greeted him, unable to keep the nerves from her voice.

"It's going to be all right, you know."

She smiled bravely.

"Are you ready?"

Girding her strength, she nodded. "Yes."

His movements were careful and deliberate as he began removing the bandages. She was accustomed to the process. The only difference today would be that she would finally look in the mirror.

Grace held her breath as the final bit of gauze was

removed. She saw a spark of joy in Noah's eyes and felt a leap of excitement. Then his eyes filled with incredible sadness.

At least she finally knew. Releasing her breath, Grace battled her disappointment as she accepted the mirror he extended.

Closing her eyes, she reached deep inside for courage. Finally ready, she pulled the mirror closer and opened her eyes.

She stared at her image. Her full, unabridged image.

Puzzled, Grace wondered if she was imagining what she saw.

Hesitantly her hand strayed to her face.

Noah's voice was gentle. "The two small marks will mostly fade in time."

She moved the mirror even closer. The marks were so small she could barely see them, just their red stain. Unable to understand Noah's saddened reaction, she glanced up at him. "Why aren't you happy about the results?"

"But I am," he reassured her.

"Then why do you look so incredibly sad?"

He searched her face, his expression tight. As though pulling himself from some faraway place, he cleared his throat. "Because now you're ready to return to your life in Houston."

"No, I'm not!"

"But you and your fiancé have waited for this day."

"Patrick isn't an issue." She met Noah's eyes, her own pleading for him to understand. "What we had is over—and has been for a very long time. He returned to Houston two nights ago. Patrick is part of a past life I've left behind."

"After he sees you, he won't let you go."

"Is that how you judge a woman?" Suddenly it was terribly important to know this about him. "Simply by her looks?"

"The eyes are important," he replied solemnly. "For they reveal the heart." He stepped an inch closer. "And the lips, because they speak either in kindness or to wound."

"And the nose?" she asked, entranced by his words.

His lips edged upward. "Very important. I can't abide snobbish women."

"And how do you see me?"

He swallowed and she glimpsed tenderness in his eyes. "Ah, Grace. Woman of infinite beauty, that's an unfair question."

Her heart pounded so loudly she wondered that he didn't hear it. "Why is that?"

"Because you're leaving soon."

Finding a confidence she thought was lost forever,

Grace put her heart on the line. "Can you think of a reason for me to stay in Rosewood?"

His eyes locked with hers. "Do you need a reason?"

Solemnly she nodded, praying he could read her thoughts.

He touched her newly healed cheek. "How about the fact that I love you?"

Heart thrumming, she felt a surge of newfound hope.

Regret infused his face. "But that's not enough."

"Why?" she cried.

"You can't be happy in my little one-horse town." He met her gaze, his eyes shining with naked love. "And I can't ask you to give up everything for me."

"I've grown to love Rosewood and the people here nearly as much as I love you." Her lips trembled and her eyes filled. "And because of that, I've also found my way back to God. I know now that you were right about opportunities. The Lord blessed me with an opportunity greater than I could ever have wished for." She reached up, tenderly touching his jaw. "And He led me to you."

Noah's hands folded into her hair as he pulled her close. "Grace, I love you so much. I see your smile each day when I wake, I dream of your changeling eyes each night as I sleep. But I never thought you could be mine. Are you sure?''

''More sure than I've ever been of anything. You *are* my life now, Noah. And my love.''

Noah tenderly fitted his lips to hers, his soul filling with thanksgiving, unable to believe this lovely, wounded bird was to be his.

Grace took hold of the dream that she had once despaired of, grasping it close to her heart. She would keep it there, tenderly securing it along with her love for this noble man. Her knight, she realized with new wonder. Who would stand by her forever.

The sunlight that streamed through the examining-room window seemed to glow as though cast from heaven itself. And together their hearts took flight—not away, but upward on the wings of a love destined to last for all time.

Epilogue

The church that had become hers radiated with hope and love. Massive bouquets of flowers decorated the altar. Their fresh scent mingled with that of newly lit tapers.

Grace looked out at the crowded pews of wedding guests. She was still unable to believe how many friends she had made in the town that was now her home.

Noah's family had welcomed her warmly as one of their own. Along with Ruth, they provided her the family she had always dreamed of.

It was a perfect day for her wedding, filled with sunshine that etched an elaborate tapestry as it pushed past the stained glass windows.

Joyous organ music resonated in the aged, beautiful sanctuary. The mood of the music fitted the jubilation of the day, the joy Grace knew would fill their union.

So much had happened while the wedding arrangements were being made. Grace's former employer had decided to become a permanent endower of the Rosewood Medical Foundation. Although he maintained he could never replace Grace, he had embraced the foundation with his usual generosity.

Robert had excelled on his scholarship exam—surpassing all their expectations. His father had found employment and the entire family was doing much better. Grace still tutored Robert, though. He would always be special to her—her first student. He had been enormously pleased when they'd asked him to be an usher for the wedding. Grace noticed that he had taken special care escorting Noah's parents to their pew.

With Noah's encouragement, Grace was securing her teaching certificate. It had been scary at first, returning to school. But she enjoyed the challenge nearly as much as substitute teaching. She could hardly wait until she became a full-fledged teacher.

The music swelled again and Grace felt her throat tighten with joy. It would only be moments now.

Cindy, her matron of honor, walked up the aisle, taking her place opposite Michael, Noah's best man.

Ruth patted Grace's arm. "I think they're about to play our song."

Grace smiled, pleased that Ruth was walking her down the aisle. It might be unorthodox, but Ruth had been both mother and father to her. They had shared so much. It was only right that they also shared the beginning of this newest path.

"I don't know if I would have agreed to give you away if you weren't marrying Noah," Ruth added, her eyes glistening.

"You're gaining a son, not losing a daughter," Grace told her gently, wanting Ruth to know she had been so much more to her than an aunt.

Tears spilled onto Ruth's spare cheeks and she reached for her already rumpled handkerchief. "Thank you, child."

The music swelled once more. Grace used her now fully recovered hand to squeeze Ruth's arm. "I think that's our cue."

The guests rose as Grace and Ruth moved up the aisle. But Grace didn't watch their faces. Her gaze was fastened on the man soon to be her husband. He stood tall and handsome.

And her heart called out to him.

Noah's deep blue eyes signaled his reply.

Her smile widened.

They reached the front of the church.

"Who gives this woman?" Katherine asked as the notes of the organ faded away.

Ruth squeezed Grace's hand one final time, said, "I do," then stepped away.

With no one left between them, Noah took her hand in his. And Grace savored the rightness of his touch.

Then they both gazed at Katherine, who smiled at them before beginning the age-old words.

Sunbeams pierced the stained glass windows, punctuating each sacred promise.

"Will you take…from this day forth…"

Grace and Noah steadily repeated their vows.

When the words *in sickness and in health* were to be echoed, Grace felt the emotion lodge in her throat, her voice tremulous as she spoke.

But Noah's eyes filled with promise.

Lips trembling, she didn't take her gaze from his.

"I do," Noah uttered, his strength flowing through to her.

Two such very small words. Carrying with them the promise of forever, Grace realized, blinking back the tears before she, too, repeated them.

"I now pronounce you husband and wife."

Noah lifted his hand to tenderly cup Grace's cheek.

Somewhere in the distance she heard the sighs of guests.

"You may kiss the bride," Katherine told them, her voice filled with joy.

Noah's lips gently covered Grace's, sealing them with a promise of devotion and commitment she thanked God for. Eyes misting with overwhelming happiness, she looked up at the man who was now her husband.

Triumphant strains of music flowed from the organ, seeming to reach the very beams of the old sanctuary.

"I now present Mr. and Mrs. Noah Brady," Katherine concluded.

Grace placed her hand in Noah's larger one, knowing he would always make her feel as safe and loved as she did at that moment.

"Shall we?" he asked, his gaze lingering on hers as though searing this memory for all time.

Hand in hand, they took the first step of their new lives. Walking down the aisle, they smiled at friends and family.

As soon as they passed through the double doors that led from the sanctuary into the foyer, Noah pulled Grace along with him to the empty bride's room.

Turning, he drew her into his arms. "My bride... my wife."

Without warning, her eyes misted. "I love you so."

Again he cupped her cheek, gazing deeply at her. ''I had to fix one thing in my memory.''

''What?''

''The color of your eyes on the most important day of my life.''

She felt her heart stutter with a wealth of emotion for this rare and wonderful man. ''And?''

His look was tender. ''The color of heaven.''

''One thing about me will never change, Noah. My love for you.''

He lifted her scarred hand, one she had chosen to leave as it was, a reminder of what had brought her a new life, a renewed faith, a love like no other.

Gently he kissed that hand. ''Forever, Grace. We have forever.''

It was a gift from above, one they could share, as matchless as the golden sunlight that fell around them.

Her hand clasped in his, they walked from the tiny room to greet their friends and family. Connected by touch, by hearts, by spirit, their smiles reached out to all those watching.

And like the sunshine, their love was radiant. Also matchless, a joy that reached to the sky and beyond.

Forever.

* * * * *

Dear Reader,

This story called out to me because it's one of change. Like many of you, I feel surrounded by change—in our world, our country. I'm not usually the first one in line to embrace change, so it made me wonder about a woman who would have to deal with change in every aspect of her life.

Even as the familiar comforts us, I wondered, could change possibly comfort us even more?

I invite you to join my journey of promises, friendships and, most especially, love. And I hope that all your changes are joyous.

Warm wishes,

Bonnie K. Winn

Love Inspired

BLESSINGS

BY

LOIS RICHER

She wasn't what he'd expected…but surgeon
Nicole Brandt is just the temporary assistant
Dr. Joshua Darling requires. The widowed dad
desperately needs help with his patients and his
three rambunctious daughters. But can Nicole make
him see she is his perfect partner in medicine—and
the perfect wife and mother for his family?

Don't miss

BLESSINGS

On sale October 2003

Available at your favorite retail outlet.

Take 2 inspirational love stories FREE!

PLUS get a FREE surprise gift!

Mail to Steeple Hill Reader Service

In U.S.
3010 Walden Ave.
P.O. Box 1867
Buffalo, NY 14240-1867

In Canada
P.O. Box 609
Fort Erie, Ontario
L2A 5X3

YES! Please send me 2 free Love Inspired® novels and my free surprise gift. After receiving them, if I don't wish to receive anymore, I can return the shipping statement marked cancel. If I don't cancel, I will receive 4 brand-new novels every month, before they're available in stores! Bill me at the low price of $3.99 each in the U.S. and $4.49 each in Canada, plus 25¢ shipping and handling and applicable sales tax, if any*. That's the complete price and a saving of over 10% off the cover prices—quite a bargain! I understand that accepting the books and gift places me under no obligation ever to buy any books. I can always return a shipment and cancel at any time. Even if I never buy another book from Steeple Hill, the 2 free books and the surprise gift are mine to keep forever.

113 IDN DU9F
313 IDN DU9G

Name _____ (PLEASE PRINT) _____

Address _____ Apt. No. _____

City _____ State/Prov. _____ Zip/Postal Code _____

* Terms and prices are subject to change without notice. Sales tax applicable in New York. Canadian residents will be charged applicable provincial taxes and GST. All orders subject to approval. Offer limited to one per household and not valid to current Love Inspired® subscribers.

LI03

©2003 Steeple Hill Books

An Accidental Mom

by

Loree Lough

Becoming Mrs. Max Sheridan was all Lily London had wanted, but he'd married another. Now Max is back—with his motherless son—and the dream is revived. But Max is afraid that Lily won't be prepared to take on a ready-made family. Can Max and Lily learn to trust in God's leadership... and in their love for each other?

Don't miss

AN ACCIDENTAL MOM
On sale October 2003

Available at your favorite retail outlet.

Visit us at www.steeplehill.com

LIAAM